Anna Wintour Biography:
The Life and Career of the Fashion Icon

"Create your own style... let it be unique for

yourself and yet identifiable for others."

- Anna Wintour -

By Ryan T Cox

TABLE OF CONTENTS

INTRODUCTION

Anna Wintour is one of the fashion industry's most powerful leaders today. She is the Editor-in-Chief of Vogue, one of the world's most prominent fashion publications, as well as the Chair of the Metropolitan Museum of Art's Costume Institute.

Anna Wintour has made important contributions to the fashion business, including the creation of new fashion trends and designs, the promotion of rising designers, and the advancement of many industry professionals' careers. She has also established numerous fascinating projects and events to promote the fashion business, such as the annual Met Gala fashion festival and the iconic documentary "The September Issue," which each year exposes the Vogue magazine creation process.

Anna Wintour, on the other hand, has received criticism and controversy, including criticism for her attitude and management style at Vogue. Yet, her career has spanned many years and continues to grow today, and she is widely regarded as one of the world's most influential fashion icons.

Family Roots

Anna, who was born on November 3, 1949, was a healthy baby with a mop of straight, lustrous dark brown hair and clever, dreamy grayish-green eyes set in a beautiful, little oval face. She was slow to speak, and when she did, she spoke little, and her parents believed she was a shy and distant flower. Anna was born just weeks before the conclusion of years of garment rationing in war-torn Britain—and clothing and fashion would become her passion.

The tiny child would have a lot to live up to as the first daughter in a family of two sons, whose father came from a military family and had become a steely, ambitious newspaperman. She was the second child of Charles Vere Wintour and Eleanor Trego Baker Wintour, born in London after the Nazi bombs and rockets had stopped raining death and destruction. James Charles, who was born two and a half years before Anna, was the other postwar kid.

Gerald Jackson, born almost a decade before Anna, was the Wintours' true pride and joy, the one to which the others would be compared.

Charles Wintour was confident that Gerald would follow in his footsteps as a journalist. The father had given the fair-haired kid a Harrods toy printing kit for his eighth birthday, replete with various faces of miniature rubber type with wooden blocks to set them in, a messy black ink pad, and a sheaf of blank newsprint. It was his favorite gift of all. Gerald produced a small newspaper, a diary about his small world, and proudly delivered the first copy of the Wintour Daily to his father, a souvenir Charles Wintour would remember for the rest of his life.

Eleanor Baker, an American called Nonie, met Wintour at Cambridge University in England in the fall of 1939. The twenty-two-year-old Bostonian, who had a prettier sister named Jean and went to a luxury ladies' boarding school in Connecticut called Westover, had just graduated from Radcliffe.

She had tried to travel to England as a correspondent for a little weekly newspaper, The Daily Republican, in Phoenixville, Pennsylvania, owned by a close family, but when that failed, she enrolled at Newnham College, one of Cambridge's two institutions for women. "It was just something to do—Nonie had no particular attachments to England," says her American relative, Elizabeth Gilkyson Stewart Thorpe, known as "Neal," who went on to become a major women's magazine editor in New York. Nonie Baker, who was noted for her sharp tongue, critical demeanor, and liberal ideas, aspired to be a writer or journalist. Instead, she would marry one and commit her life to social service.

Arthur M. Schlesinger Jr., a mutual acquaintance and Peterhouse College, Cambridge, classmate of Wintour's, acted as Cupid for Nonie and Charles, describing him as "a pleasant-looking young guy with glasses, a rather saturnine smile, and an impressive air of professional efficiency."

Nonie Baker and Schlesinger had known one other since his undergraduate days at Harvard, where her father, Ralph Baker, was a respected professor at the Harvard Law School and Schlesinger's father was a well-known historian. During the war, Baker also worked as a co-counsel for the US agency that confiscated immigrant property. Her parents were well-to-do, having met at Swarthmore College and "thee and thou" in a Quaker wedding ceremony. Baker had built a fortune as a corporate attorney in Philadelphia, representing clients such as the Pennsylvania Railroad, before heading to Harvard to teach. His wife, Anna Gilkyson Baker, after whom Anna Wintour was named, was a charming, matronly, slightly ditzy society girl from Philadelphia's Main Line who was known to leave her children in the park and not realize it until she got home.

Schlesinger, like his father, went on to become an eminent Pulitzer Prize-winning historian, author, and trusted adviser to Jack and Bobby Kennedy in the 1960s, while his best friend, Charles Wintour, went on to become one of Fleet Street's most powerful, creative, respected, and feared newspaper editors.

Neal Thorpe claims that Schlesinger "was very much in love with Nonie" at one point in Boston and "wanted to marry her," which Schlesinger rejects years later. "I was fond of her," he admits, "but she did not physically appeal to me." Schlesinger recalls Nonie from her early days in Boston and London as "intelligent, humorous, and critical." She had a keen eye for other people's flaws and was generally critical of the world."

In retrospect, he believes Nonie was crucial as a form of "self-protection because I believe she was quite vulnerable." But she was also a lot of fun to be around as long as you weren't the target."

While Charles Wintour appeared to Schlesinger to be "the perfect Britisher," he had really spent the previous summer traveling across America and was labeled a "Americanophile."

When they met, Wintour was the editor of Granta, a student Cambridge weekly that was a cross between the Harvard Crimson and the Lampoon. Schlesinger criticized the publication. With "brisk but rather enigmatic kindness," Wintour welcomed Schlesinger's suggestions and encouraged him to write pieces and attend editorial board meetings. A bogus byline was eventually invented by the two. A. Case—A. Glandular Case—appeared on occasion in stories critical of other university publications.

Wintour was a shrewd businessman who took Schlesinger under his wing and introduced him to everyone who mattered. Because of his chum, Schlesinger got to know "more campus big figures" than he ever did at Harvard. Wintour, according to Schlesinger, was "a man after my own heart—inquiring, skeptical, sensitive to interpersonal relationships and politically competent at shaping them, adaptable, and robust."

Wintour, who possessed a cunning and bad-boyish demeanor, took Schlesinger to meet his family in Dorset. While there, he showed his guests around some of the most intriguing local landmarks, like the Cerne Abbas. It was the figure of a naked male with a twenty-six-foot erection carved out of a hillside, which Wintour included on the itinerary because he liked giving his passengers a good fright.

Schlesinger adored Wintour and reciprocated his loyalty by introducing him to Nonie Baker, who "hit it off right away."

"They became a couple two or three months after they initially met," Schlesinger recalls. Nonie was quite fascinating to Charles, and she was undoubtedly elegant. She had a patrician air about her, and she seemed to represent a fine, healthy American girl. Charles was charming and witty, but he was also in command. I wouldn't say he was really attractive. He wasn't a Ronald Coleman." Schlesinger wasn't exactly a beauty, either, so the two had that in common as well.

About the same time that Wintour and the Baker girl began dating, Schlesinger began dating a friend of Wintour's, Anne Mortimer Whyte, the daughter of a member of Parliament and Winston Churchill's private secretary. Wintour made it a point to know all the right people.

The two couples—Charles and Nonie and Schlesinger and Whyte—frequently double-dated. Schlesinger cast Wintour and Whyte in starring roles in a collegiate production of Shakespeare's As You Like It.
With war imminent, the two couples spent their final days at school driving about in Wintour's convertible with the top down.

It was a "careless, beautiful" time, according to Schlesinger.

Charles and Nonie married on March 13, 1940, in the little parish church of St. Mary the Less near the university, in a simple ceremony performed by a university chaplain. Their witness was Wintour's father, retired Major General Fitzgerald Wintour, a career military man. Gerald Jackson Wintour was conceived when the happy couple settled at a local motel after their wedding. It was a love affair and marriage during the war; Charles Wintour had already enlisted and was in uniform. There was no time to waste.

Mrs. Wintour kissed her husband, a second lieutenant in the Royal Norfolk Regiment, goodbye and flew to Boston to be with her family and have the baby a little more than a month before her due date. With the war raging, the young parents-to-be reasoned that the child would be safer in America, out of harm's way, while London was being blitzed by German rockets and bombs.

Nonie gave birth to Gerald, a healthy boy, in New England Baptist Hospital on November 20, eight months and one week after the Wintours' wedding.

She returned the infant to her family's apartment in Barrington Court on trendy Memorial Drive on the Charles River, where she breastfed him.

Despite the obstacles, Gerald grew into a strong, independent, rough-and-tumble young man.
He had no idea who his biological parents were for the first four years of his life.

Nonie Wintour, a real-life Mrs. Miniver, chose to leave Gerald with her parents and return to England to be near to her husband and do anything she could to help in the war effort over there, with London in flames and her groom in the thick of the Battle of Britain.

"She abandoned the baby because she was so in love with Charles," recounts Patti Gilkyson Agnew, Nonie's first cousin, whose father was Anna Baker's brother. "Uncle Ralph and Aunt Anna nurtured Gerald until he was about four years old."

The Bakers became Gerald Wintour's surrogate parents for the duration, which Agnew and other American relatives felt was an emotionally challenging position. Nonie mailed home photographs of herself and her husband as often as she could, which the Bakers would show to Gerald, gently telling the toddler that those strangers in the photographs were his real mommy and daddy so that he would recognize them when they came to retrieve him in the final days of the war.

When that moment arrived, it was an extremely emotional scenario, remembers Patti Agnew. "When Nonie and Charles arrived to claim Gerald, Ralph and Anna were crushed. "They treated him as though he were their kid," her sister, Neal Thorpe, observed.

Wintour survived the war, working mostly in intelligence and eventually ended up in General Dwight Eisenhower's headquarters in Paris. He saw little battle but was awarded the American Bronze Star and the French Croix de Guerre, both of which are normally presented to those who have really experienced action. Years later, Schlesinger, who had also served in Europe and had even spent some time with his friend as fellow officers, was startled to discover that Wintour had gotten such high military awards, according to a longtime friend and newspaper colleague. "He never informed me."

With the war over, the Wintours returned to London and purchased a nice contemporary-style property on Cochrane Street in the upper-middle-class London neighborhood of St. Johns Wood.

Wintour started as a secretary for one of the world's most powerful, shrewd, demanding, and authoritarian press barons, Max Aitken, better known as Lord Beaverbrook, on London's Evening Standard in 1946. Wintour was a rising journalist who would soon become one of Beaverbrook's most devoted and inventive fair-haired boys.

The Wintours' future appeared to be extremely promising. Charles and Nonie had James, and then Anna, the future Vogue editor in chief, in fast succession.

Yet, eighteen months after Anna was born, a catastrophe struck the family, with long-term emotional consequences for Anna, her siblings, and especially her parents.

The third of July, 1951, was a beautiful day in London. Nonie Wintour had allowed Gerald, ten, to ride his two-wheeler to the Hall School, a private preparatory school for boys in Hampstead, where he was a student, because there was no rain forecast. Since he was five years old, the child had been riding a two-wheeler. Gerald left home with his book bag and wearing the school uniform, a pink blazer and cap, because his father had "full faith in his skills" and allowed him "to take his own route" to and from school because "he was an exceedingly cautious driver." He never came back.

The youngster was hit by a car while pedaling home in the afternoon on Avenue Road, a big route surrounded with trees and enormous mansions. He was flung into the air, landed on the hood with such force that the windshield was cracked, and collapsed senseless onto the street. "I wasn't in a rush, and I didn't see the youngster until I was a few yards away," the driver stated at the inquest. "I went to pass without blowing my horn." I didn't expect he'd change his mind. I didn't see him put his arm out." According to witnesses, the youngster had no idea what hit him.

Nonie Wintour went to New End Hospital in nearby Hampstead after receiving the call, but she was too late. Gerald died of a fractured skull and severe injuries twenty minutes after arriving in the emergency room. His death was eventually determined to be accidental.

His mother was inconsolable. She dialed a pay phone and attempted to contact her husband, who was meeting with Beaverbrook at Cherkley Court, his vast, secluded nineteenth-century gray stone estate with some thirty bedrooms in the town of Leatherhead in Surrey, roughly two hours from London at the time.

What happened next, of which there are several versions, became part of the whispered Fleet Street folklore around Charles Wintour's life, and was one of the reasons he was regarded by many as an editor with icy water coursing through his veins.

Paul Callan, a respected senior London journalist who began his career working for Wintour, is one of many who heard what he considers to be a credible account of what transpired that sad day.

"Charles was Lord Beaverbrook's secretary at the time, and he was receiving dictation from him when the butler came in and requested to speak to Charles," Callan recalls. "Charles stepped outside with the butler, who informed him that his son had been murdered." Charles returned to the room, said nothing to Lord Beaverbrook, and resumed taking dictation. Nobody knew what drove him to do it. Charles wasn't a monster, but he was cold-blooded."

Alexander Walker, who would go on to become a well-known film critic at the London Evening Standard, the publication Beaverbrook eventually gave Wintour to oversee, discovered that he had actually called Nonie after receiving the urgent message concerning Gerald. "But, Charles had determined to complete his employment with Beaverbrook before coming home," Walker explains. "When he told his boss what had happened to his kid, Beaverbrook was astonished by how bravely and businesslike Charles had handled the news, and that he was able to continue working." It established Charles's reputation at Beaverbrook."

"There's no question that the death of the kid put Charles into the arms of Beaverbrook," recalls Milton Shulman, who started in journalism with Wintour soon after the war and eventually worked under him as the Evening Standard's esteemed theater critic.

Whether Wintour hurried to his distressed wife's side or stayed by his boss's side, the death of their firstborn was terrible, and the events surrounding the tragedy cast a permanent shadow over the Wintour family.

"Charles' actions when the son was slain divided the marriage," Callan observes.

"The big tragedy of Charles's life was that he, like a lot of Beaverbrook's editors, was a creature of his proprietor," Walker, who was close to both Charles Wintour and especially Nonie, says. The death of the boy ended the Wintour marriage forever, and Charles became a very frigid, aloof character. It's a heartbreakingly sad narrative.".

Nonie Win-tour, furious with her husband and depressed about her son's death, packed up tiny Anna and James and flew to Boston to be with her family and be consoled. Some believed the marriage was over.

Wintour and Beaverbrook became friends when his wife was away. Beaverbrook required bright, young editors for his newspaper network at the time, so the two met regularly. So he put Wintour to the test, instilling him with his numerous conservative views, having him write editorials to see whether he could present them with Beaverbrook's point of view, and promising him an editorship someday.

Nonie Wintour and Anna and James returned to London at the end of that horrible summer of 1951. Her and her husband reconciled, but their marriage was never the same.

Anna grew up in a dreadfully depressing and chilly environment.

Nonie Wintour had two more children in quick succession after Gerald died, hoping that a larger family would warm the icy air. Anna became pregnant less than a year after the tragedy, and on February 3, 1953, she received a sister, Nora Hilary, with whom she would never be close because they were so different: Anna would grow into a beauty and a fashionista, thought of as frivolous by the rest of the family, while Nora was plain looking like their mother, academically inclined, and a political activist.

Nonie became pregnant again a year later, and on November 1,1954, two days before Anna's fifth birthday, she gave birth to another boy, Patrick Walter.

But it was Anna who took the place of Gerald as the fair-haired child in the eyes of Charles Wintour. But he adored all of his children, Anna quickly became and remained his favorite. Yet Anna was the one of the four surviving Wintour children who resembled him the most—driven, ambitious, inventive, chilly, and always with her eye on the prize.

Anna would go on to become the most famous of the Wintour children, considerably outperforming her father as a prominent editor. Only Patrick became a journalist out of the other three. James and Nora, like their mother, were societal do-gooders and led relatively calm and steady lives. Nora married a Red Cross worker in Switzerland, while James worked in public housing in Scotland.

Apart from her hatred toward Charles for his response, or lack thereof, to the murder of their firstborn, Nonie began to loathe her husband for working for Beaverbrook, whose political and social ideals she strongly opposed.

"Nonie was very left-wing," Milton Shulman adds, "and she always loathed Charles's sacrifices working for Beaverbrook, compromises that you had to make if you want to be editor of a right-wing journal."

Shulman, like Beaverbrook, was a Canadian, therefore the publisher liked him for reasons other than his ability as a young journalist. Beaverbrook requested Shulman to become deputy editor of the Manchester Daily Express, one of the publications in the Daily Express chain where Beaverbrook tried out new editors for bigger posts, in the early 1950s, according to Shulman. But Shulman, a member of Canada's Socialist Party, declined the position because he disagreed with Beaverbrook's political views. "I told him I'd have to give up either my work on the paper or my political beliefs." That was something I didn't want to do. It was my only exam for the position of editor, and he never asked me again."

Yet when Beaverbrook invited Charles Wintour to take the job in Manchester, he gladly accepted, much to his wife's disgust. "Nonie never moved up there with Charles," Shulman claims. "She remained in London with the kids."

Nonie was "extremely disappointed in Charles's commitment to the Beaverbrook line, which was very much opposite to her own instincts and ideas," according to Shulman's wife, journalist Drusilla Beyfus Shulman, who socialized with the Wintours. She wasn't sympathetic to Beaverbrook's principles and was pretty naggy about them to Charles. Nonie and Charles were uninterested in one other's points of view."

Beaverbrook was inspired by Wintour, and when Anna was five years old, her father was appointed deputy editor of the Evening Standard, and in 1959, at the age of forty-two, he was named editor in chief. With his remarkable eye for recognizing bright editors, writers, and columnists, he turned the publication around. He also got the moniker "Chilly Charlie" because of how severe, distant, and demanding he was. As his authority expanded, he became a womanizer, adding to the marital strife in the Wintour household, particularly affecting young Anna.

Nonie Wintour became a passionate, some say obsessed, social worker throughout the 1950s; they attributed her intense participation in the tragic situation of others to her liberal Quaker upbringing. Her first employment required her to work with persons who were deemed mentally incompetent by the authorities. She later worked with foster children and adoptive families. For a while in the early 1950s, the writer in her emerged, and she tried her hand at freelance film criticism for Time and Tide, an intellectual and political British journal whose contributors had included Virginia Woolf, D. H. Lawrence, and Emma Goldman throughout the years. She has the potential to be cruel. She termed one picture a "preposterous plot," another a "lachrymose love romance," and a third a "airy French confection." . . a stale piece of sponge cake." She rarely gave two thumbs up in the dozen or so reviews she posted.

Anna went inside, grew even more introverted and reclusive in a home filled with so much sorrow, and had no known close friends.

She was as quiet as a church mouse at North Bridge House School in Hampstead, a loner who blended in. Her parents' divorce had clearly had a negative impact on her. Coupled with the sadness that had descended in the aftermath of her brother's death, her father, whom she adored, was rarely around, preoccupied with Beaverbrook and his career as an editor.

In September 1960, Anna was eleven years old and enrolled at London's prestigious Queens College, which wasn't so much a college as it was a posh middle and high school catering to such wealthy young heiresses as Christina Onassis, girls who arrived each morning in chauffeur-driven automobiles. According to one of Anna's classmates, it was a school that "trained ladies to be educated wives" at the time.

Though Queens College had a lot of cachet and was very chichi, Anna disliked it and hated having to put up with the extremely strict discipline. Students were not authorized to speak in some areas of the facility and were forced to stand and stop speaking when a teacher entered the room, according to the guidelines. The school was kept so frigid (warmth was thought to be detrimental for discipline) that a classmate had frostbite on her feet.

Anna despised the school uniform, which consisted of a pinafore with a long-sleeved white shirt, striped tie, and cardigan sweater.

With all of the rigidity and regimentation, a student described Anna as "willful, resentful, and highly complex." "Anna didn't seem to have a desire for a lot of girlfriends. She didn't seem to have any close friends, and if she had, she didn't seem to keep any."

"When you meet Charles Wintour, you'll be turned off by his somewhat chilly appearance, but when you get to know him better, you realize it's only the tip of the iceberg," Susan Summers, who went to Queens and later worked for the Evening Standard, was reportedly informed. . . . The difference was that he was truly liked by his employees, whereas she was not. A well-liked leader. She had a fairly messed-up background, and she grew up to be a very cold woman."

Anna stayed at Queens College until July 1963, when the Wintours transferred her to another luxury all-girls' school, the century-old North London Collegiate, where she was accepted on September 18, and where the students were known as "North London Clever Girls."

Swinging London

Nineteen sixty-three, the year Anna matriculated at North London Colle-, giate, an explosion of enormous proportions rocked Britain. It was dubbed a youth quake, a psychedelic nuclear blast of fashion, style, and music that quickly resounded around the world. And Anna came of age in that momentous time, infusing her with an extreme interest in fashion.

"That moment in time that Anna and I were growing up in London," Vivienne Lasky reminisces, "was just not to be replicated."

The hair—the sexy, sometimes fishy but always timeless bob—became an integral part of the look in the swinging London scene. Always on top of trends, Anna rushed to get her lush, thick, straight brown hair cut and styled in the new fashion, which became a key component of her chic image, the cut she still wore in her mid-fifties, a cut that not so coincidentally has been favored and popularized by the British dominatrix, as Anna, the editrix, would later be described by some submissive and mistreated underlings.

The bob had been around for ages, first given public attention in the 1920s when the actress Louise Brooks wore it as the character Lulu. Also a model, Brooks appeared occasionally in fashion ads exposing the bob to the masses, which helped define the flapper look. Now it would define trendy London birds in the revolutionary and exuberant sixties.

Among those whose look inspired Anna to get the bob was Maureen Cleave, one of Charles Wintour's talented favorites on the Evening Standard staff.

"Charles simply adored Maureen," says journalist Valerie Grove, one of Cleave's close friends and a colleague on the paper. "She was petite, dark, brisk, brilliant, clever, sharp, and very articulate— adorable in every way And Charles was absolutely enthralled with her. Maureen had the bob, and it became sort of her trademark.

Everybody on the paper thought that Anna copied Maureen's hairstyle and that is the origin of the Anna Wintour look.People thought Charles was expressing his adoration of Anna, and his ambitions for Anna, through his keenness for Maureen. It was really some kind of dynamic there."

In fact, Alex Walker believes that Anna's decision to copy Cleave's hairstyle was, indeed, psychologically complex—more than just her desire to be in fashion. "Charles revered Maureen, Charles was Maureen's mentor, and Anna desperately wanted Charles to cherish her, too," he maintains. "It's quite complicated, but I'm sure Anna wanted to be able to say, 'Look at me, Daddy. I look like Maureen.' Anna always desperately—desperately—sought Mr. Wintour's love and attention, and he wasn't always there to give it."

Wintour wanted a hipper, younger readership, and twenty-three-year-old Cleave, an Oxford graduate with a degree in art, was given the youth page beat—the same with-it demographic that Anna later targeted, likely on her father's advice, when she first became a fashion editor.

"Charles ran many of his ideas for me through Anna because she was keeping her eye on [trendy] things," Cleave says, looking back. "She was a hip kid, so to speak. I got in trouble once for not knowing the difference between 'hip' and 'hep.' Anna obviously told her father about that. I'd written the wrong word and Charles said it should be the other word. I knew he'd gotten the correct one from Anna."

Cleave had virtual free rein to cover the smashing rise of swinging London. The nonpareil Maureen Cleave interview became dinner table and cocktail party conversation.

Her biggest score came when she got a tip from a friend in Liverpool. "She said to me, 'I hope you realize there's a lot going on here. There's this group called the Beatles.'" The quartet had recently cut their first single, "Love Me Do," and had signed a five-year contract with a manager named Brian Epstein.

Cleave ran the Beatles story idea by Wintour, who asked Anna whether she had ever heard of them. Of course, she told her father, they're fab. The next day Cleave headed north, thinking she had an exclusive,but was disappointed when she arrived to find a competitor on the scene from the Daily Mail, who had also gotten the word to check out John, Paul, George, and Ringo—known as "the Fab Four"—and this new Mersey Beat.

The gentleman from the Mail didn't have a chance, though. Lennon preferred Cleave as their interviewer, which she attributes to her bob. "I had a fringe like the Beatles. They liked me from the start because of my hair. I guess they felt we could relate."

Beginning on Thursday, October 17, 1963, and continuing for three days, the first major interview with the Beatles ran in Charles Wintour's Evening Standard. That same day the Beatles were at the Abbey Road Studios recording what would quickly become their first American number one hit, "I Want to Hold Your Hand."
Cleave's series, pushed by Anna's highly competitive editor father, who ran the story idea by his with-it teenage daughter who kept her eye on who and what was in and out, had helped to catapult the most successful singing group in music history.

Anna's bob had helped, too. If Cleave hadn't been wearing it, the Beatles might not have been so friendly and open, and she might not have gotten their story. In any case, it didn't hurt.

In its 1963 incarnation, the bob was the brainchild of Vidal Sassoon, who had a shop in posh and fashionable Mayfair that had catered for centuries to London's upper classes and royalty. Sassoon's guinea pig was the fashion designer and sometimes model Mary Quant, the epitome of the with-it, mini-skirted swinging London chick. She was thrilled with the cut and decided to have all of her models given the bob by Sassoon. A British Vogue editor, attending Quant's show, was overwhelmed. "At last," she wrote, "hair is going to look like hair again."

Other trendy haircutters soon jumped on the bob bandwagon, such as Leonard of Mayfair, where Leslie Russell gave Anna her very first bob. "Anna was about fourteen, fifteen when she came in. She had hair way past her shoulders, like Jean Shrimpton's. She said she saw photos in [British] Vogue of some cuts that I did, and I remember she came in with a picture she'd torn from Vogue. And so I cut her hair, and it was the haircut of the time, which everyone was getting—the straight hair, the long fringe, the same bob she has today."

Mainly, Anna chose Leonard of Mayfair over Sassoon because two of her idols got their bobs there—Maureen Cleave, and a kicky nineteen-year-old former ten-pound-a-week secretary named Cathy McGowan, who overnight jumped to the forefront of the British pop revolution as the trendy host of a top-rated music television program Ready, Steady, Go!, Britain's version of American Bandstand. Virtually every teen from London to Liverpool—and Anna was no exception—tuned in early on Friday evenings, 6:07 P.M., to be precise, before they went out clubbing. The show's energized motto was "The Weekend Starts Here!"

Adolescent Anna idolized Cathy McGowan, who dressed in the latest boutique clothing and makeup trends and embodied the vocabulary, attitude, and sensibility of mid-sixties bustling London. Every week, Anna would walk away from the television knowing what to purchase, where to get it, and how to wear it.

"Cathy was one of my clients," Leslie Russell explains. "She had the bob, and Anna had read in a magazine or newspaper that I'd trimmed Cathy's hair, which was another reason she came to see me." It was ideal for Anna. And continues to do so. She has excellent cheekbones, which are ideal for the appearance of the moment. Undoubtedly, back then, she had excellent, lustrous, thick light brown hair that hung straight with a bit of blow drying to turn the hair under a little. Anna appeared to be in her sixties."

Russell never forgot Anna's look: short, short miniskirts; low-heeled, pointed shoes; tight tank tops; and minimal makeup—"some eyeshadow and mascara, but that was about it." She didn't have red lips or makeup on. She didn't require it.``

Anna began undergoing scalp treatments and purchasing special-formula hair products from a bespectacled man named Philip Kingsley, who took hair very seriously, in addition to going to Leslie Russell to have her hair cut. He intended to be a doctor, but visits to his uncle's hair salon piqued his interest in hair care. Instead of attending medical school, he trained as a trichologist, a specialist in hair and scalp issues. In the early 1960s, he established a one-man practice in London.

"Charles Wintour came to see me because his hair was thinning," Kingsley explains. "And he saw me throughout his life." 'You should start taking care of your hair when you're young,' he urged Anna. 'When Anna initially came to me as a teenager, she didn't have much wrong with her, but I started treating her, too. I get people's hair in the greatest condition possible so they may do whatever they want with it. It's the same as going to the doctor."

Anna dutifully used Kingsley's shampoo, which had a formula based on the texture of her own hair, as well as his proprietary hair tonics and conditioners over the years. Kingsley also advised her to take a lot of yeast medications, which produced constipation.

Anna kept seeing Kingsley, who had begun a clinic in New York in the mid-1970s, after she went there to begin her ascent. Kingsley thinks that stress is terrible for hair, and as Anna ascended through the ranks of the high-pressure fashion magazine industry, hopping from one anxiety-ridden fashion editor's position to another, her tension grew and she needed his assistance.

"The frequency with which I saw her was determined by how stressed she became," Kingsley explains. "Her hair didn't respond as it should have when she was under stress, and sometimes Anna was under more stress than others." Kingsley kept track of Anna's good and poor hair days and examined her hair's health on a regular basis, depending on the highs and lows of her anxiety.

Anna was one of Kingsley's first clients, joining Cher, Jerry Hall, Mick Jagger, Ivana Trump, Sigourney Weaver, Kate Winslet, Candice Bergen, and Barbra Streisand on the list.

Apart from her hair, Anna worked hard to keep her skin in good condition as a teen. She devoured her gospel, the American magazine Seventeen, which had copies she took from Vivienne Lasky, who had a subscription, to learn how to combat pimples, acne, and blotches—as well as how to deal with other teenage girl difficulties. She went to an elite salon on Baker Street, fancier than Elizabeth Arden, for facials on a weekly basis, convinced she would have poor skin and preoccupied with keeping it clear.

"Her skin was fine," Lasky says, "but she went to the salon once a week for a preventative."

While Anna was stylish and fashionable, she was fiercely critical and snarky, and she made fun of those who weren't. "Anna was quite concerned with her appearance. 'My God, look how obese she is,' she would say to another girl. . . Take a peek at her face. . . "Look at that girl's dreadful, curly hair," recalls Lasky, who had curly hair and was the focus of her best friend's harsh tongue at times. Despite the fact that both wore glasses—were Anna's costly tortoiseshell granny glasses—she mocked Lasky's poor vision. "Anna didn't always wear her glasses," Lasky explains. "She could manage without them, though she'd occasionally ask me who someone across a crowded room was." But because my eyesight was so impaired, she'd be quite judgmental of me and unpleasant when we were horseback riding or playing tennis. I had difficulty seeing the ball. I couldn't keep up with her. She has the potential to be cruel."

Anna was abrupt and sardonic when she was a teen, attributes she got largely from her father but also from her mother, who was known for her critical and sarcastic demeanor.

Anna's hostility was intentional and insulting, making Lasky and the others she targeted feel bad.

"If there was one thing I despised about Anna when we were kids, it was her nastiness on the phone," Lasky says. They never said goodbye to her entire family. They'd simply hang up on you. It was inevitable with Anna. 'All right, I'll see you later.' Click. There will be no farewells.

"'It's the rudest thing, no civility,' my mother would remark, and my mother adored Anna." I challenged her. 'What's the deal with not saying goodbye? 'And she replied, 'Well, is there really no point? We're done talking. How can you be upset about that? Nobody else does that,' I remarked. People will think you're strange if you try to make friends with them. You're the only person I know who does that.' She didn't seem to mind."

Even greater slights left Lasky heartbroken and with a bad taste in her mouth, both about herself and their friendship. Lasky, unlike Anna, was an eater, and Anna took pride in the fact that she was always skinny. Anna, for example, purchased small clothes gifts for Lasky. Yet there was always one huge stumbling block. Everything was oversized, including a custom-made Regency ball gown with lavender and white stripes that Lasky could barely fit into.

"These are things that my mum noticed. 'How could your best friend buy you something when it's always too small?' she used to say. "The dress Anna bought me, I couldn't get into it because the arms were so tight." Anna also got Vivienne a costly patchwork quilt skirt at Liberty's, one of London's grandes dames. "It didn't fit like anything else," she adds, "I think I squeezed into it once."

Lasky's mother was a former ballet dancer and model from Prussia, an exotic cross between Audrey Hepburn and Greta Garbo, according to her daughter. Brigitte Lasky, a fashion plate who converted to Judaism for her Jewish husband and became a U.S. citizen, was a fashion plate with whom Anna bonded, spending almost as much time with Mrs. Lasky as she did with her own ordinary mother, who was absorbed with her social work. "Anna was very fond of my mum," Lasky explains. "She considered herself to be the cat's meow and saw herself as a role model."

Yet, Brigitte Lasky believed Anna purchased the small sizes on purpose and intentionally to humiliate and mock her daughter. Unlike Vivienne Lasky, who was a little chubby, Anna was slender, but she had enormous bones and had to buy larger sizes and have them taken in. While Lasky believed Anna looked "wonderful" in some items, such as later in Chanel, she thought she looked "terrible" in evening gowns back then and now, "because her elbows, wrists, and knees are too wide." She reminds me of Calista Flockhart and Lara Flynn Boyle. That appears to be painful."

Anna was well aware that her friend preferred succulent, thick lamb chops. She even taught herself to make them to Lasky's liking so she could gloat while watching her eat them. "Anna would prepare my favorite dish. She'd then simply sit there and watch me eat. 'Oh, Anna, I don't want to be a model,' I responded, and she said, wagging her finger, 'You know, Vivienne, we don't want to grow too chubby.' My mother claims I would always come home from those dinners feeling a lack of self-esteem. She stated that I did not return confident and happy."

Anna offended her buddy by mocking her weight and putting her on the spot by demanding, "Why don't you have more self-control?"

" Lasky's humble reply was, "Life is too brief. . . Dieting constantly makes me grumpy.' Yeah, that sends a message. I wasn't that dumb. 'Anna invites you to dinner, makes your favorite dish, buys your favorite cheesecake, and she's flitting around, but did she eat anything?' my mother used to say. 'Mom, you know she didn't,' I said. My mother assumed she was nasty. 'I don't believe that of her,' I'd remark. She adores me. 'She's my best buddy,' I say.

Alex Walker, a favorite of Charles and Nonie Wintour on the Evening Standard team, frequently socialized with his editor. He was invited to their cocktail and dinner parties—Charles specialized in creating martinis that had people reeling—and stayed overnight at their country estate in West Farleigh, a hamlet in Kent. Then he met young Anna, who he described as an "absolute monster" who "didn't mind pushing on [her] own ideas on whatever anyone else said, especially in that household."

Walker assumed Anna would do or say things just to hurt him. He describes her as a complex mixture of wicked cinema characters such as Rhoda Penmark from The Bad Seed, Vida Pierce from Mildred Pierce, and Eve Harrington from All About Eve. Walker loved cinematic parallels, even if they were potentially overstated, as a movie critic and serious historian of Hollywood greats.

"I'd spend the weekend with Charles and Nonie," he recalls. "Anna was maybe fourteen or fifteen, and she had a horse." I'd hold the long harness as I led her around the pasture, rather than galloping around it. 'I think I've had quite enough of this, Mr. Walker,' she'd say when she'd finished riding. 'Please help me down.' I was astonished by how mature she was—far more mature than her age. There was definitely a future editor in the family."

Anna was obsessed with horses at the time, and she persuaded her father to abandon his important job at the Evening Standard and. take over as editor of the local Kent Messenger in order for her to enroll at the local stables with hopes of becoming a stylish, miniskirted veterinarian.

"Even as a child, she had her father's coldness," Walker says. "She reminded me a lot of her father." Anna possessed a maturity well above her years. She was more than just self-assured. She was aristocratic. She was not a boisterous child. Her behavior was pretty subtle back then, consisting of being stiffly courteous but not paying much attention to you. What she did was done on purpose."

But Anna had no tolerance for impolite behavior that interfered with her life, and she was especially irritated by people who were late. "Anna could be really impatient," says Vivienne Lasky. "She was, in fact, a perfectionist." In that way, she reminded me of Martha Stewart, as she was always in command. Anybody being late was incredibly nasty to Anna, and she cut people off if they didn't arrive at the exact time specified—at least not anyone terribly important to her. 'Oh, we're not going to encounter them again,' she'd add conclusively. 'They are untrustworthy. We'll just go it alone. "What is the point of meeting somebody if they are late?"

London Party Girl

A hustling, ambitious charmer of a Fleet Street "hack" named Nigel Dempster, over a decade her elder, was more in line with the type of guys Anna was drawn to. Dempster was digging up dirt at parties for London's Daily Express gossip section when he started seeing sixteen-year-old Anna.

Anna was drawn to Dempster's good looks and debonair demeanor, as well as his expanding circle of expensive acquaintances and the wealthy riffraff he drew. Vivienne Lasky, on the other hand, left with the impression that he was "smarmy and slimy," while Charles Wintour's blood ran cold when he learned that his daughter was dating "a gossip hack."

Other aspects of Dempster piqued Anna's interest, such as his alleged lineage: he claimed to be a descendant of one of the two families that founded the powerful Elder Dempster Lines, a shipping company that controlled West African trade beginning in the late nineteenth century and was on par with the Cunards. There was even a glossy in circulation of Dempster in white tie and tails at the age of twenty, which he said was a family society shot.

Whatever the reality was, Anna was interested, and Dempster, who was always on the lookout for new opportunities, saw both journalistic and romantic possibilities in her. They became a couple. They shared many interests and values, including power, fortune, and celebrity. "A number of males wanted to go out with Anna because they wanted to court favor with Charles Wintour—and that included Dempster," writes journalist Paul Callan, who later had his run with Dempster.

Through Anna, Dempster fantasized of becoming Charles Wintour's big gun: he wanted to be the most well-known and well-paid gossip writer of his generation. The latter would happen, but without the assistance of Anna's father, who felt he was a moron.

Lasky couldn't see what Anna saw in Dempster even after years of trying. "He was so authentically British," she adds, "backstabbing and spiteful." "I didn't believe he had a moral fiber in his body." . . "That harlot is charming to your face."

Anna became a fixture of sorts on the London party and club circuit through Dempster, who was beginning to hobnob with the highbrow and lowlife of British society and celebrityhood, not quite the Anglo version of a Hilton sister but regarded hot stuff and identifiable to the cognoscenti (Fleet Street reporters who also made the scene and who knew who her father was).

Anna watched Ready, Steady, Go! on Friday night before going out. And she was in Biba or Mary Quant, two of the hippest boutiques, first thing Saturday morning, looking for the kind of kicky, seductive outfit Cathy McGowan had worn on the tube the night before. Saturday nights, she drove to the Laskys' spacious duplex apartment overlooking Hyde Park for dinner, with the time set aside at eight o'clock to watch The Forsyte Saga.

She'd trot off to the clubs around eleven o'clock—never, ever sooner because it wasn't fashionable—usually starting her rounds at midnight at Dempster's main haunt, Annabel's, which was packed with a mix of real and self-styled aristocrats and a bit louche gambling crowd. Anna enjoyed the men's attention, devoured the gossip, and kept a close eye on the women—what they dressed, how they wore it, what was in and what was out.

She was a regular at the Ad Lib, in Leicester Square, which had a reputation for being a hangout for London's hottest dollies, a club where almost everyone in the balcony overlooking the dance floor was high.

Anna didn't do drugs, despite the fact that marijuana, cocaine, LSD, and whatever else you could snort, inhale, or shoot to get high was all around her, everywhere she went.

"Anna was always too in charge to be interested in drugs," Lasky says. "She was horrifically healthy," she adds, adding that Anna didn't even drink at clubs and instead nursed Coca-Colas, but she wouldn't refuse Veuve Cliquot if presented by a gentleman.

Anna frequently went to Dolly's on Jermyn Street, which drew a hip crowd of journalists and rockers, and she was a regular at Sibylla's, on Swallow Street near Piccadilly Circus, which became known as the Beatles' disco because George Harrison owned a tiny percentage of the club. The club's special pre-opening night was spectacular, with an all-star lineup of celebrities including all of the Beatles, the Stones, Cathy McGowan, Julie Christie, and Mary Quant, among others. It was the kind of club where the proprietor thought it was successful only if you couldn't get in, therefore it was Anna's kind of place, and she was there for the premiere with Nigel Dempster.

"When Anna was fifteen or sixteen, she had this downtown London life," Lasky explains. "London was a hive of clubs, concerts, and never-ending parties." She traveled to places where it was trendy to be seen and seen. She didn't require much rest. She was bursting with enthusiasm.

"She preferred clubs, clubbing, and dancing to the Beatles or the Stones." Anna didn't attend rock concerts or have a crush on anyone in pop music."

Yet Anna did have a thing for a gorgeous late-fifties star who was more her speed—the actor Laurence Olivier, whom she saw at least a dozen times in Shakespeare's Henry V. As most girls her age were pursuing Mick and Keith, Anna started seeking Olivier. She frequently skipped school, carrying a satchel of clothes with her and changing into something provocative in the ladies' room of the subway station near the office building where Olivier had his production firm. She'd camp out in the lobby for hours in the hopes of meeting him. This went on for months, but she was never successful, and she eventually gave up her search.

Nothing seemed too risqué for sixteen-year-old Anna, who became delectable arm candy for Dempster, who once boasted that his nubile girlfriend's breasts were "large" and "quite delectable." On July 1, 1966, Anna partied the night away with Dempster and hundreds of other sybarites, hedonists, and celebrities at the five-story swingers' paradise, overseen by Woody Allen as a favor to Hugh Hefner "She'd attend to the opening of an envelope," observes Vivienne Lasky, but in this case, it was a celebration of half-naked Bunnies spinning roulette wheels and turning cards for oil-rich Arabs, British playboys and their birds, and the typical turnout of Euro trash. The crazy antics continued late into the night in the Playmate Bar, the disco, and intimate gatherings in members' rented private rooms.

An Evening Standard photographer was on hand to picture Anna shaking hands with Hugh Hefner, who was dressed in pajamas. The photographs were shown to Anna's father the next day by a gleeful photo editor. "That didn't go over well," Dempster recalled.

Charles Wintour didn't mind Anna's independence, but he did object to her dating Dempster. Brian Vine, a former London Daily Express New York bureau chief, observed Anna and Dempster together at the Playboy Club's launch. Dempster told him a few days later that Charles Wintour burst when he called for his daughter at Phillimore Gardens.

"Nigel said Charles was really upset," Vine recalls. "I think Nigel had to always cover the fact that they were seeing each other." "Charles Wintour was a pretty traditional and powerful editor, and he couldn't see his daughter dating such a scurrilous gossip hack." Nigel was unsuitable for the Wintours."

Yet, Anna was intrigued by the flashy world Dempster opened up for her, and their relationship lasted seven years, according to Dempster.

"Dempster loves to say he had [a romance] with Anna," London Daily Mail gossip columnist Peter McKay claims. "Dempster relates a story about sitting on a sofa in the Wintour home drawing room with Anna one evening when he looked up to find these two scuffed suede shoes beneath the pair of doors to the room." Charles [Wintour] had arrived home unexpectedly, but instead of entering the room, he stood silently outside eavesdropping. Dempster claims he had to conceal the romance from Wintour, who had the power to fire him."

Brian Vine heard a similar story from Dempster, with a few elements changed. Dempster stated he had to duck into a closet in that scenario because Anna was afraid her father would burst into the room and discover them together.

Many who knew Dempster believe the relationship was not romantic. "Dempster would be terrified because he aspired to be a journalist," Vine observes.

"Anna was extremely young and Nigel thought she was terribly lovely," says Dempster's first wife, Emma de Bendern, who comes from a titled household. "I'm sure that was just a dating thing," she insists. "When I married Nigel, he brought Anna to Spain, where my mother had a small property on Mallorca and I lived." She came to spend the long weekend with Nigel. She wouldn't go out in the sun since she had the most beautiful transparent skin, and she sat under an umbrella to avoid getting any sunlight. She was like a porcelain doll, flawlessly manicured, silent and unassuming, hidden behind the fringe of her perfectly trimmed bob, and her physique unbelievably skinny—but with astonishing, underlying resolve.

"She didn't seem to have a personality, and I didn't sense any sexiness in her." I simply remember Nigel being really protective of her, almost like a father figure to her. There was no romance, in my opinion. But perhaps I was duped, and that was a cunning deception to avoid raising my concerns. Yet there was no indication that he was having an affair with her. It didn't feel that way."

If there was anything intimate going on, one would expect Anna to tell her best friend about it. Yet she remained mum. "Anna never talked about sex or relationships," Vivienne Lasky adds. "We weren't Sex and the City. And Anna is very British, quite private, and not overly sentimental. She'd never discuss what had happened between her and a male."

By 1971, Dempster had advanced from lowly legman to second in command under Paul Callan, who engaged him to write on his new Daily Mail "Diary" column. Callan quickly recognized he'd made a huge mistake by hiring Dempster, who attempted to steal his job. According to one source, "Dempster stabbed him. It was classic material. He saved all of his good stories until Callan was gone, then produced them in a way that made Callan appear bad."

Whatever Callan thought of Dempster's career maneuvers, Anna is reported to have admired his ruthless tactics. They shared a similar philosophy: "Go to the top any way you can," according to a journalist who knew both of them.

Shopgirl Dropout

If there was a watershed moment for young Anna Wintour, it was the day her father called the Evening Standard's fashion editor, Barbara Griggs, into his office and asked, "I wonder if you could do me a big personal kindness?" "Charles, I'd be delighted," Griggs, who had been covering fashion for years and had previously worked at British Vogue, responded. What should I do? "

"Well, my daughter Anna believes she wants to do something in the fashion business," he added, sounding a little nervous. Could you take her out to lunch and give her some advice? Of course, I'll pay for the lunch."

Years later, Griggs reflects, "I don't think Charles was big on fashion, and I don't think he wanted it for his favorite daughter." At the time, he hoped for more for Anna."

Griggs brought Anna to lunch and found herself sitting across from "this really self-possessed child—extreme self-possession, which is remarkable in someone her age." She found Anna to be very focused and left their meeting believing that this girl will go far. "It appeared to me that she required no instruction and that she'd carve her own way quite effortlessly."

Griggs called Barbara Hulanicki, the owner of Biba, one of London's hottest boutiques, the next day, still following through on her editor's request, and asked if she had any part-time openings for a very savvy and confident schoolgirl whose father happened to be the powerful editor of the Evening Standard. Anna was a regular customer who wore the designs Hulanicki promoted—knee-high boots, tight shirts, and miniskirts—and Vivienne Lasky is convinced that Biba and its fashions affected Anna's passion with clothing.

The boutique rose to prominence in London's sixties fashion scene, influencing how girls dressed on the street. Hulanicki devoted close attention to the cut of her outfits, giving them a couture aspect, so that any female who wore her designs appeared slim. Overnight, Biba's customer base shifted from working-class girls to pop stars, actresses, aristocrats, and all the young fashionistas like Anna who wanted the "look." An expert at promotion, Hulanicki shrewdly designed outfits specifically for influential trendsetters like Cathy McGowan and the highly visible pop singer Cilla Black. Julie Christie wore Biba in the film Darling. Twiggy, the legendary model, was always dressed in Biba designs.

Biba's hot mail-order catalog utilized photographers like Helmut Newton—a favorite of Anna's when she became a fashion editor—to create photos that combined innocence and knowingness, which was, in reality, Anna's image in the eyes of men during the 1960s and 1970s.

Hulanicki recalls receiving a call from an Evening Standard fashion editor acquaintance, Barbara Griggs, who said, "Oh, might the daughter of Charles Wintour come and have a vacation job?" Hulanicki said yes right away—a prominent editor's daughter as a shopgirl couldn't hurt business—and engaged her to work on Saturdays and holidays in her Kensington Church Street shop as well as at a Biba branch in touristic Brighton on the English Channel. Hulanicki would frequently accompany Anna and a few other girls on the one-hour train excursion. They worked in the shop all day and returned that night.

"Anna would have been about fifteen or sixteen years old," Hulanicki says, "and she was very young, very nice, extremely pretty, and very, very quiet, but I got a feeling her intellect was definitely a little bit better than fashion." Anna hailed from a well-educated family, although the majority of the Biba girls did not. She was out of the ordinary. She, on the other hand, became one of the girls who were learning the boutique business."

Hulanicki was fascinated with Anna and kept a close eye on her. "I could see she was taking everything in," Hulanicki says of Anna, who appeared bashful and frightened. "Anna was into fashion, but

Biba was the place to go." Boutiques were the most important sites back then. . . "Everyone wanted to work for them."

Hulanicki recalls Anna, who was paid roughly $15 per day, as "very fat" in comparison to the other Biba females, who were even skinnier than Twiggy. Yet, this could be due to eating problems or, worse, narcotics. And most of them were at least eighteen years Anna's senior. A lot of them led incredibly wild lives: some became addicts or alcoholics, while others died tragically in a series of car accidents, most likely intoxicated or stoned, victims of swinging London's excesses.

To say the least, Biba was a spectacle.

Joanna Dingemann, Anna's age and also a "Saturday girl," later a Biba manager, a Paris model, and a fashion school teacher, says Anna stood out from the lovely crowd even then—an elegant and, she adds, very furry vision. "She used to wear fur—a full-length fox coat—at a time when wearing fur was just becoming unfashionable. . . . It was simply falling out of favor, not in a political sense as it is today, but simply in terms of fashion. Yet she was wrapped in it. Anna took her own path."

While Charles Wintour used his good name and influence to obtain Anna her boutique job—and it wouldn't be the last time her father's authority would help her advance—his hope at the time was that Anna wasn't serious about fashion as a career.

"Charles and Nonie assumed it was merely a phase," Vivienne Lasky observes. "It was exactly what she had anticipated them to say. Her parents couldn't understand it, but Anna had a lifelong obsession with clothes. By sixteen, she was all about clothes, fashion, fashion."

Her life had been consumed by the London fashion revolution. Years later, Anna reflected, "You would have had to be living up in Scotland underground to not have been influenced by it."

Brigitte Lasky provided Anna with encouragement for her fashion enthusiasm that she did not receive at home. Lasky, who wore couture, and Anna had continuous chats about clothes and style, which Anna had never had with her own mother.

Nonie Wintour, as a social worker, wore thick glasses, avoided makeup, and dressed conservatively—"like a working person, Talbot-sy," adds Vivi-enne Lasky. "Nonie reminded me more of Hillary [Clinton]." . . I won't bother, I'll put on the next navy blue suit. Nonie wore navy a lot." Later, when she became interested in fashion publications, Anna would buy clothes for her mother to make her look more sophisticated.

Unlike Anna, none of the other Wintours were fashionable, and they all dressed simply. "Anna despised people who were ill-dressed," Lasky recalls. "We'd be on Bond Street eating tea at some chic spot, and she'd make comments about everyone." She was really critical. Everyone has to be flawless. She remarked on their attire. 'How can people behave in such a way? They never look in the mirror, do they? '"

Anna once purchased an expensive Dior dress shirt for her brother Jim, who wore it wrong, allowing it to hang out of his pants. Anna merely rolled her eyes and shook her head.

"It's incredible that Anna came from that background," says Drusilla Bey-fus Shulman, a former British Vogue editor and Wintour family acquaintance. "They were all horribly clothed. They were hilarious. Nora's clothing was awful—all of them were pathetic. Nora is a pretty plain girl who suffered greatly as a result of being a plain girl in Anna's shadow. She was always the ordinary sister, whereas Anna was wonderfully beautiful and always looked great.

"It appears that Anna was convinced of the practically psychic power of garments as early as the age of twelve." She always looked dreamy when she went out with her lovers, whether she was thirteen or not. I remember seeing her in a really dazzling white coat and boots, maybe vinyl, on her way to Switzerland for a vacation. She had to have been fourteen, and she was stunning."

Anna's parents, according to Shulman, never understood her early love with fashion. She compares their reaction to that of parents who learn their child is a musical genius. "Where did it come from?" Who can say? Why do these incredible qualities emerge? They simply do. That comes from no one in the Wintour family, for sure. Natural talent is her secret."

Because of their close relationship, Anna confided in Brigitte Lasky, one of the few women who had ever joined that enchanted circle. Surprisingly, Anna noted that her mother seemed more interested with, and affectionate toward, the foster and adoptive children in her case files than with her own flesh-and-blood children. Anna angrily referred to the children in her mother's case files as "Nonie's kids," and while she rarely displayed emotion, she plainly felt bitterness toward her mother since she wasn't more of her focus.

"That made Anna feel like a second fiddle," Vivienne Lasky explains.

Lasky, who was friends with Anna's mother for many years, believes Nonie Wintour was completely happy by her work with children. "Maybe Nonie was compensating for the death of her first child, whom she couldn't save, by throwing herself in and saving other people's children."

Anna had the same desire for Charles Wintour's attention—a father figure and mentor to his newspaper staffers but not always present for his own daughter.

Years later, she admitted, "I was never alone with my father when I was a child." We were simply too numerous. He was the one we were afraid of, but he wasn't harsh. He's modest and nice in that manner, but he notices everything and you always know what he thinks." He was much more devoted to his work than his wife. Anna claimed she didn't see him much because of his newspaper and recalled "interrupted holidays" if wars erupted or people were slain. Anna claimed that her parents were frequently absent and that she had spent a significant amount of time as a child with nannies and au pairs.

"Nonie had a work ethic, and Charles had an amazing work ethic," Lasky explains. "They shared the same interests and stayed true to those interests." Anna, too, possesses an exceptional work ethic."

When Anna did see her father, he built excitement, telling her which celebrity or prominent politician had come into the office that day or the huge story the paper was working on. He gave her the same rush of adrenaline that caused him to rub his hands together and exclaim, "Hah! " in the Evening Standard workplace when juicy tales like the John Profumo-Christine Keeler sex scandal rolled in thick and fast like they did in the 1960s. He made Anna feel powerful, as if she were an insider. She thought it was fantastic to have inside knowledge of something that would make news the next day.

"Nonie and Charles adored their children and were greatly admired by them." Yet there was never a particularly warm family atmosphere since Charles' attention was usually elsewhere. You can't edit a paper like the Evening Standard while also thinking about what Anna wants to do in the afternoon. "It didn't exist," Drusilla Beyfus Shulman observes. "I won't call Charles an absentee father because he was obviously worried about his children, but he was at his desk extremely early in the morning, stayed all day, and dined out with friends in the evening." He didn't have much time left for Anna."

Anna found a surrogate in Vivienne Lasky's dictatorial father, the esteemed Melvin Lasky, who wasn't easy to be around because he could be very caustic and cruel.

So what about Anna? Anna was the best in Lasky's opinion. He seemed enthralled and enchanted by his stories about celebrities he knew and instantly recognizable writers like Mailer, Eliot, Auden, and other major names whose pieces he edited and revised. Anna would sit at the table, seemingly enthralled, but occasionally peppering him with questions. Did he know this individual? Had he met that person before? Do great authors ever object when you correct them? Anna was aware that her father's style was to keep his hands away from his reporters' copy until absolutely essential. "Some will inquire, 'Did you make any changes?'" 'Lasky said to her. "Anna, you have to give them the impression that's how they wrote it."

While the Wintours granted Anna enormous independence—her own apartment, freedom to meet older men, and clubbing until all hours—Charles and Nonie were most concerned about her lack of enthusiasm in education, as seen by her attitude at North London Collegiate. Charles, from Cambridge, and Nonie, from Radcliffe, were educational elitists who desired that she graduate and attend a proper university. The Wintours had intended for Nora, Patrick, and James—all academic high achievers—to attend Oxbridge and had begun to put pressure on Anna. "I remember them talking about it with Anna and telling her, 'You'll be the first not to go,' and of course they expected her to follow in their footsteps," Vivienne Lasky said.

"Charles was the family's brilliant thinker," Drusilla Beyfus Shulman observes, "and Anna was, well, attractive." Charles, the family's brilliant thinker, was always suspicious of Anna's intellectual abilities."

The Wintours' tug of war with Anna over her education ended in 1966. Anna, who was about to turn seventeen, had had it with North London Collegiate. It would be an item of clothing, the miniskirt, that would enable her formal schooling to come to an end.

Although Anna was arrested for minor transgressions during her three years at North London, she was frequently let off the hook, owing to the fact that the headmistress, Dame Kitty Anderson, was a friend of Charles Wintour's brother-in-law, Lord James of Rusholme, a well-known educator. Anna felt entitled because of Dame Kitty's connections to the Wintours. All of that changed in July 1965, when the headmistress retired and was replaced by Madeleine McLauchlan, who began to make Anna's life miserable. "She was frigid and hard," Lasky says, "she acted as if she had a stick in her ass." The entire school was transformed. Things grew quite tense. No one passed the tests that were offered. "Everyone was nervous."

There are variations to the account of Anna's unexpected demise of her school career, just as there are to Charles Wintour's handling of the devastating news of his first child's death. The only thing that has been documented is a basic notation in the North London Collegiate School records. Anna "was here from 1963 to 1966," according to historian Elen Curran, and nothing in the records indicates that she graduated. While she is one of the most well-known and successful alumni of North London Collegiate, she has left little trace of herself. "Unfortunately, we do not have any further information about Anna Wintour in our archive," Curran says.

Anna walked into North London Collegiate for the last time in July 1966, at the age of sixteen, wearing a skirt that reached her knees. McLauchlan noticed her and was determined to make an example of her.

"Anna was always six months ahead of fashion," Charles Wintour famously observed of his daughter's graduation. "In North London Collegiate, Anna was doing well until a new headmistress arrived and noticed her miniskirt." She propped Anna up on a table and ripped her hems. So Anna had to ride the tube home in a torn skirt, which effectively ended her interest in academic life."

According to Drusilla Beyfus Shulman, the incident not only killed Anna's "passion" in school, but also prompted her to leave North London Collegiate a year early. According to her version of events, "Anna trimmed her gym skirt so that it was above the knee—I mean well above the knee—which was a really predictive thing to do in terms of fashion." Those incredibly low skirts have only recently arrived. 'Look at this girl!' remarked her French mistress as she hauled Anna up onto the desk. She is unworthy of this prestigious institution, and she is simply concerned with clothes. She is free to go! 'As a result, Anna departed North London Collegiate and never returned.

"Anna is rather pleased with the story. It is absolutely compatible with her character—she is quite self-possessed and also has this sense that she is doing the right thing."

Whatever happened, Anna had completed her formal education at the age of sixteen, leaving in a huff over having to follow the rules. Her last day on the job was July 27, 1966.

"She was defiant and had plainly had it with school," Lasky says.

Anna's parents' greatest fear had been that she would not attend college; they had never anticipated her to drop out of high school.

"I guess I went the other way," Anna said years later. "When my sister left a message on my answering machine, she always made this joke." She inquired as to whether I was at the hairdresser's or the dry cleaner's. As a result, I was always the bimbo."

The Wintours were now concerned about Anna's future and had realized that her innate fascination with fashion was more than just a phase, as they had previously assumed. Her father's hopes for daughter to follow in his footsteps were also thwarted since she refused to work in the newspaper industry, getting her delicate hands stained with printer's ink. Anna has remarked that she has never attempted to "prove anything" to her parents. Her passion for fashion was all-consuming, but what she would accomplish with it remained vague and unfocused.

"I'm not a particularly reflective person," she once admitted, reflecting on that time. "As a result, I didn't have a wonderful life plan."

Finding Love at Harrods

Anna's class at North London Collegiate was finishing its final semester in the fall of 1967. Vivienne Westwood follows in the footsteps of Nonie Wintour.

Lasky was accepted to Radcliffe. But Anna was uninterested in the usual signs of young adulthood, such as attending college or leaving the family home. She pretended to be an adult in the Wintours' basement apartment.

Instead of pursuing academics, Anna was accepted into a Harrods training program, where she worked in every department with the objective of becoming a buyer. She was assigned to learn all aspects of the jewelry industry at one point, and she sold scarves and accessories in the Knightsbridge emporium's funky teen boutique, her favorite department.

Because it was a work-study program, Anna also attended classes at a mediocre Trafalgar Square fashion school at the request of her parents, who believed that even in fashion, she should have some sort of official education. Anna nearly set fire to the place following an allegedly failed classroom experiment. According to Anna's later account to Vivienne Lasky, she combined and matched a couple of materials with some chemicals, lit a match to them, and whoosh. Anna's enrollment was short-lived; she quickly lost interest in what the school had to offer—"you either know fashion or you don't," she claimed when she dropped out.

Anna's main interest, aside from fashion, was men—attractive, older achievers.

"She had a lot of lovers," her father once said. "She was actually practically pursued around the house by Indian statesman Krishna Menon," Wintour said, without saying whether he thought Krishna Menon's fatal heart attack in 1974, at the age of seventy-seven, was caused by his alleged feverish pursuit of his comely daughter. He also never revealed that he and Krishna Menon were classmates at Cambridge and that the tale he told a London publication could have been made up.

"I'd see Anna about and wonder, 'What do these guys see in her?'"

"'Paul Callan recalls. "There was something mysterious about Anna, hiding behind her hair, looking out, and appearing so shy." Of course, no one realized that behind all of that was this ferocious girl, extremely Wintourian, intentional, everything planned, very brilliant."

While working at Harrods, Anna met and began dating Peter Gitterman, who was thought to be the stepson of the brilliant conductor Georg Solti, music director of London's Royal Opera House and later principal conductor of the London Philharmonic Orchestra, giving the young man access to London society.

"He wasn't very attractive, but he was intriguing and intelligent," Lasky adds. "He obviously admired Anna and had a huge crush on her."

Anna was particularly drawn to Gitterman's celebrity connections, a select group that included Rudolf Nureyev and members of the royal family such as Princess Margaret's husband, fashion photographer Antony Armstrong-Jones, better known as Lord Snowdon. Anna met Peter Sellers, Vidal Sassoon, and Mary Quant, among others, through Gitterman. Anna's involvement, on the other hand, presented a conundrum. While she was smitten by him, she couldn't care less about his big loves—the symphony, opera, and ballet.

In a conundrum, she sought advice from Lasky. "Anna was insecure since she didn't know anything about any of those topics." 'He genuinely likes you, and he'll probably appreciate teaching you, but you should read up,' I told her. "Since she liked and dated this guy, she quickly learnt opera and ballet." 'I'm going to the opera!' she said the next thing I knew. What should I put on? '"

The relationship faded, and so did Gitterman, who vanished from the scene. Anna left the Harrods training program about the same time.

For a time, she dated Robin Blackburn, a good-looking left-wing figure who lectured at the London School of Economics on the Cuban revolution and wrote for the New Left Review. Charles Wintour reportedly detailed Anna's plans to accompany Blackburn to an anti-Vietnam War demonstration. "I heard her patter down the steps, turn, and go up again after having spent two hours contemplating what to wear to a protest," her father recalled. 'Daddy, am I for or against Cambodia?' she said as I opened the door. '"

While Wintour made fun of his daughter and had long since realized she wasn't cut out for rocket science, Blackburn claims he didn't think she was as much of a jerk as her father made her out to be.

"I imagine he found this part a matter for remark contrasted to Anna's later evolution, or with Charles Win-own tour's then-politics," Blackburn says years later. "Her father's implication that Anna didn't know anything about politics isn't my memory of the matter," says Blackburn, who went on to become a professor of sociology at the University of Essex. Anna had made a short visit to the United States and returned with a gift of several books about the Vietnam War, which he found quite useful, though he acknowledges that Anna may have purchased the books based "on someone else's advice."

Anna and Blackburn remained friends after their romance ended. In the 1970s, he became a member of her social circle, which included Patrick Wintour and up-and-coming literary darlings like novelist Martin Amis and hard-drinking journalist and later American TV talking head and Vanity Fair scribe Christopher Hitchens, who wrote editorials for the Evening Standard under Charles Wintour.

Anna had purchased the Vietnam books for Blackburn while visiting her mother's favorite first cousin, Elizabeth "Neal" Gilkyson Stewart Thorpe—the Stewart and Thorpe representing her first and second husbands—who was then an articles editor at Ladies' Home Journal, where she handled personality pieces and cover stories, and conducted interviews with celebrities and politicians ranging from Carol Burnett to a Supreme Court chief justice. She had also worked as a fiction editor at Redbook.

Anna, who had dual citizenship due to her mother, had planned her first solo trip to New York to hunt for jobs on Seventh Avenue and to look into fashion colleges. Thorpe had only met Anna, a first cousin once removed, on a few occasions when she was a toddler.

Thorpe was excited for Anna's visit. With her first marriage's two sons away at boarding school, she offered Anna one of their bedrooms and settled in for a good time in the hopes of getting to know her better.

Anna's maturity, refinement, and style astounded her. "My God, I was so struck by how she looked, how she handled herself, how gorgeous she was," she said, but she also thought her cousin's daughter lacked intellectual depth and had a shallow interest in fashion. The magazine editor and the prospective magazine editor, as it turned out, did not get along.

"We had no relationships because of magazines," she explains. "Anna's only passion was fashion, and I was completely uninterested in fashion, so we didn't have much in common." She was interested in apparel, whereas I was engaged in reading and writing. Anna was drawn to magazines because of her passion in fashion, not because of her interest in publications."

Thorpe did her hardest to entertain Anna, but she was met with a hostile, chilly attitude, and things swiftly deteriorated.

Thorpe was left with a foul taste in his mouth after Anna's departure. Nonie Wintour's other favorite first cousin, Patti Gilkyson Agnew, who lived in New Mexico, claims Anna's lack of thanks for her stay left Neal feeling hurt and mistreated. "Neal will never forget Anna never said anything more than 'thank you for letting me live with you for a month and eat supper with you.'"

The visit highlighted Anna's icy relationship with her mother's American relatives. Some of that was probably certainly owing to the water that separated them. Even after Anna moved to New York permanently, she made no attempt to connect with any of them. "She never ever contacted me," Thorpe adds.

Anna's sole other encounter with her American family—an fascinating and imaginative bunch—was in the early 1960s, right before she enrolled at North London Collegiate. Nonie accompanied Anna, James, Patrick, and Nora to a reunion of the Gilkysons and Bakers at Squam Lake, a magnificent wildlife area in central New Hampshire, with her sister, Jean Read, an editor for New American Library. The Gilkysons had rented a set of summer cottages there, and family members from New Mexico, California, and Pennsylvania had joined Nonie and her children.

Anna met several of her relatives, including two who had come from Hollywood with their parents. "Terry" Gilkyson III was a well-known composer and pianist. One of them was Nancy Gilkyson, Anna's second cousin, who eventually worked as a Warner Bros. executive. "Nonie and my parents that summer had a lovely time and laughed all the time," records. During that summer, I wrote to Anna for approximately a year, and then we lost touch."

Eliza Gilkyson, Anna's younger sister, describes Anna as "so gorgeous, beautiful, yet detached" at the reunion. She was cold and unfriendly. That was the single occasion that our paths intersected. I never saw or met her again." She went on to become a singer of her own compositions about sex, drug addiction, and death. Johnny Cash and Tony Bennett have recorded Eliza and Nancy's father's tunes. He co-wrote such successes as "Marianne" and "Memories Are Made of This" with his band, Terry Gilkyson and the Easy Riders.

Few people in Anna's circle had any idea she had such remarkable American relations. She never mentioned them and pretended they didn't exist. It seemed as though she was embarrassed or denied her mother's American ancestry. At the time, Anna thought herself to be completely British.

Family Affairs

Anna had been hearing well-founded tales about her father being a womanizer since she was fifteen. Subsequently, references to his extracurricular activities began to appear in the "Grovel" gossip column of London's snarky satirical magazine Private Eye.

The piece linked him to a married woman and made fun of his lack of knighthood, which he felt he deserved.

"It was obvious to an old friend his interest in her had a certain sexual tinge," writes Arthur Schlesinger Jr., who had been introduced to the woman via Win-tour. She was energetic, seductive, and bright, and Charles was a powerful editor at the time. Womanizing was not a major motif in his life, but he enjoyed clever, attractive women and I'm sure slept with them. "Charles had a British reserve about things and was not given to confessionalism."

According to the paper's then-correspondent in the nation's capital, Jeremy Campbell, who had long heard the stories about his boss's escapades, Wintour once turned up with the beauty at the Evening Standard's Washington, D.C., bureau, staying with her at the Madison Hotel. Nonetheless, Wintour attempted to debunk the reports. "Charles told me, 'Whatever you hear, she's my traveling partner and nothing more.'"

Campbell's reaction? "I suspended belief."

Alex Walker, who became close to Nonie Wintour before, during, and after her marriage, feels that tensions between her and her husband peaked in the late 1960s and early 1970s. "The kids were growing up. Nonie was very active in her social work. As a result, Charles became increasingly interested in the feminine delights that a number of ladies afforded him.

"Charles would never have discussed any of this." He would have considered such a breach of trust in marriage. If he had any true confidantes, it was most likely the other women he was with. He became the type of husband who relaxes with a mistress to relieve the stresses of family life."

Wintour "riffled through secretaries at the paper, one after the other, and poor old Nonie was at home," a female former Evening Standard reporter recalls. "He was cold and cruel to her. They threw fantastic cocktail parties, but they were really unhappy together."

Anna knew about her father's wanderings from what she saw and heard at home, from Private Eye, and from the whispers in the circle in which she ran. She was always very secretive and never mentioned the gossip.

"She was quite reserved in that regard," Jennifer Hocking observes. "She wouldn't have discussed it, because Anna was not a gossipy type with whom you could sit and have a wonderful dish."

According to Vivienne Lasky, her father's philandering was difficult for her to deal with or understand intelligently. "Anna suspected that some of the women reporters at the Standard weren't merely protégées. Anna had a feeling something was wrong. One was invited to the country, was included in a lot of activities even with Nonie present, and he frequently took her to parties if Nonie didn't want to go.

"Anna couldn't go to her mother or father and ask, 'What's this all about?'"

'She's so very British,' observed Lasky. "We had many discussions about our fathers being womanizers. She was aware of his infidelity and that he had protégées, and she forgave him for everything. When Private Eye initially began reporting on gossip, she personally sided with her father. That was difficult, because we both loved and adored our fathers and didn't know what to do with our sentiments. I'm not sure if it was fury. It was simply like, "What does this all mean?" "

Anna seemed to comprehend her father's philandering more than Melvin Lasky's, especially since Brigitte Lasky was fashionable and lovely in comparison to her own frumpy mother. "I recall Anna asking, 'Why would your father go any further than your mother?'" Why would he, when he has the most gorgeous woman? '"

Anna appeared to have the mindset of a Cosmo Girl, believing that it all came down to a sexy look and sex, with little understanding that relationships were far more complex.

"I admired Charles; he was charismatic and flirty," Lasky says. "And I was aware of his shortcomings. I don't want to criticize Nonie—she didn't deserve that type of treatment—but she could have gone out with her husband every now and then. Nonie was never with him anyplace. Charles would purchase Nonie jewelry on her birthday, but she would refuse it. It's as if he didn't really know her."

Nonie received an urgent transatlantic call from her sister Jean in New York on September 4, 1970, nine months after Anna had joined Harpers & Queen. Anna Gilkyson Baker, their mother, had died at the age of eighty-one. The grandmother had been widowed for over four years, since since her renowned Harvard business law professor husband, Ralph Jackson Baker, died of pneumonia at the age of 78. Baker died on November 5, 1966, two days after his granddaughter Anna's seventeenth birthday, after spending a week in the hospital.

Anna's grandmother had been discovered dead in the Bakers' Boston apartment, where Nonie had spent her formative years. The cause of her mother's death, however, was kept hidden from other family members on the American side.

Unlike Ralph Baker, who died of heart disease and chronic bronchitis, Anna Baker died of natural causes. Anna's grandma, who had apparently been depressed for a long time, committed herself by overdosing on the barbiturate Nembutal.

Anna's maternal grandpa had prudently invested his money and left an enormous estate of $2,279,578.62 (in 1966 dollars), of which

Anna was a beneficiary. When her grandmother died, she had a personal value of $204,162.93, minus her husband's sizable trust for her, to which Anna was also an heir.

Anna celebrated her twenty-first birthday in the luxury Savoy Hotel on November 3, 1970, two months after her grandmother's death. She now had a substantial income from the family trusts, the kind of money that would allow her to take low-paying fashion magazine jobs, like the one at Harpers & Queen, and still live the high life: have chic apartments, wear beautiful clothes, drive a trendy car, spend nights on the town, and date outrageous men.

A Savvy Decision

Judith Daniels was in a bad predicament. She intended to fire Anna, but Anna refused.

It hadn't always been that way between them, and the intended axing would have to wait a few months. In reality, the two had started off well when Daniels hired Anna as a freelance fashion editor for a slick and sophisticated new magazine called Savvy, aimed at the executive working woman, in the spring of 1980.

As her romance with Michel Esteban ended, Anna re-entered the workforce, this time resolved not to let anyone or anything get in her way. But there was both good and terrible news. The job market was deplorable. She went to the better periodicals, but there was little or no interest in her or any vacancies.

She turned to Jon Bradshaw for assistance once more, who was now spending most of his time in California with his future wife, Carolyn Pfeiffer.

He conducted some investigating among his media contacts and discovered Savvy, a new start-up. This new magazine was aimed at a seemingly untapped and lucrative market: ambitious Reagan-era women armed with MBAs who were entering the worlds of business, finance, and government and needed straight talk on everything from purchasing the best spreadsheet software to selecting the most appropriate wide-shouldered pinstripe pantsuit, then in fashion, to wear to an important meeting.

Even better, Bradshaw had known the entrepreneur Daniels while she was an editor at New York and The Village Voice, and Anna had met Daniels socially at parties around town with Bradshaw. Daniels had noticed her and her wit. "I liked her," says Daniels. "She was brilliant, well read, knew about art, was terrific company, and was attractive and slender." Daniels, a sharp operator with a low-key approach, had been able to preview Savvy in New York in the late 1970s, which was fantastic publicity, because of her tight ties to the magazine's editor, Clay Felker. So it took her a few years to acquire the necessary funds and gain supporters. She'd finally given birth to her child. The first issue of Savvy was published in November 1979 but was dated January 1980.

Fortunately for Anna, Daniels had just recently begun looking for a new fashion editor to replace the previous one, the respected fashion maven and journalist Elsa Klensch, who is alleged not to have worked out. When Bradshaw called, Daniels said, he said, "What about Anna?" 'And I like to think I was wise enough to respond, 'Of course, why didn't I think of her myself?' At the time, I didn't know what Anna was interested in or doing, so we talked."

All Daniels knew was that Anna had previously worked at Viva and that she enjoyed what she saw her do there. Daniels offered Anna the job of fashion editor at their first meeting, but the position was part-time, gave no perks or benefits, and made very little money—much less, in fact, than Anna was making when she got her little rise at Viva. Anna had no other options at the time, so she said yes right away. Money was not an issue this time, but visibility was. Anna wanted another platform in New York to land a truly glamorous fashion magazine job, her hope was that someone at Vogue would see her work and entice her into the area where she thought she truly belonged.

Daniels gave Anna nearly total independence at Savvy, similar to her position at Viva, at least at first, during their honeymoon phase.

"She wasn't supposed to be in the office every day," Daniel's ads. "Anna did everything on her own." She was hired on a freelance basis. We provided her a startlingly low monthly salary—about three thousand dollars—from which she was supposed to pay photographers and herself. I didn't want to find out. It was heinous.

"But she loved business and fashion so much, and she was so brilliant at it, that she was ready to work for next to nothing." [In fact, according to another editor, Anna was only collecting a thousand dollars out of the monthly fashion allowance for herself.] I had met a lot of ladies with drive and ambition. What I was thankful for was that someone with Anna's energy and desire was willing to focus on it for me. She was incredibly kind.

"I was struck by how hard she worked, how professional and informed she was, and how much others were willing to go out of their way for her." Even back then, she had an outstanding network of top-tier photographers. On this occasion, I had complete faith in her and her judgment, and she delivered on time. She had no staff (though Anna did bring Georgia Gunn with her) and no support system, but she just understood what she was doing and did it on her own. I'm not sure where she went, how she got the garments, how she wheeled and dealed, or who she had to wheel and deal with. Savvy was a newcomer. There was no budget. She couldn't just drop the name of New York magazine."

The first layout by Anna appeared in the June 1980 edition. Alice Daniel, a conservative-looking woman with close-cropped hair, wore a buttoned-to-the-throat basic blue blouse on the cover. The profile was about an "ardent civil libertarian" who was governing the United States. The Civil Division of the Justice Department. "HOW TO GET THE TITLE YOU DESERVE," and "FALSE GRIT." were among the cover lines. YOU DON'T HAVE TO BE MACHO TO GET AHEAD," and the sardonic "TELLTALE SIGNS OF THE DEAD-END JOB" in red print.

According to Savvy's cover stories and graphics, Anna had gone full circle, from the sexiness of Viva to big-time magazine Puritanism. Anna's first contribution—the only remotely sexy feature in the entire eighty-page issue—was jammed inside, on page 65, between an essay about the literary quality of notes women write on refrigerator doors and one about various sorts of scales, tape measures, and timers readers could buy. It was named "Stripes," and it was four pages of simple images of models wearing striped belts, one-piece swimming suits, and striped shirts. Anna's byline was shared with Georgia Gunn and photographer Jean Pagliuso, who was now part of her core group, which also included exceptional shooters like Jimmy Moore, with whom she had worked since her hiring and firing at Harper's Bazaar; Guy Le Baube, who had started with her at Viva; and Tohru Nakamura.

Anna seemed like an alien to the rest of the Savvy female team, most of whom were committed feminists, or, as consulting editor Kathleen Fury described her, "pixie dust thrown in among the group, who were extremely intelligent, humorous, diligent, young, smart writers." She looked like one of us, but she wasn't. Anna floated in and out of view, weighed around two ounces, and appeared to be from another planet. You knew you couldn't get too close to her."

Fury, who previously worked for Redbook and Ladies' Home Journal, says she had the strange feeling that Anna was studying her and the others as they worked, as if observing some alien life-form, exactly as they saw her as being from Venus.

"She appeared engaged and amused," says Fury. "We weren't fashion people, and she might have admired us for our ability to use the language and style." You could see her watching us—quietly, but observantly—and it was almost as if she was standing outside of a circle of people having a lot of fun, and she was enjoying, but not participating in, their enjoyment. There was something about her that suggested, "Don't get too close."

Another editor, Patricia O'Toole, who came to Savvy with a lot of business reporting and writing expertise and used to freelance for Vogue in the early 1980s, never forgot her first meeting with Anna. "I asked, 'How are you?'" 'And she remained silent. She simply looked right through me. This struck me as a negative assessment of whatever I was wearing. My clothes do not fit even the most flexible concept of elegance. But when I read years later that she was dubbed "nuclear Wintour," I thought, "Oh, that's perfect—it squared with my experience."

Anna, like Viva, rarely if ever participated in editorial meetings, preferring to stroll into the downtown Manhattan offices of Savvy wearing tight white T-shirts and tight designer trousers, or shorts and stylish flats, and discuss her plans individually with Daniels. When the images were given, Daniels, never Anna, usually wrote the copy, and it was always done at the last minute due to Anna's ongoing trouble articulating the story's contents. Anna devised the overall plan but expected someone else to handle the details.

With all of Daniels' other obligations, Daniels was compelled to appoint a writer, Carol Wheeler, to write all of the fashion material for Anna's articles. Anna's role, according to Wheeler, was minor. "She brought the clothing in, and at some time I'd hear that the piece was going to be about summer things to wear in New York, and I'd think about what to write." Anna didn't even explain the concept to me. I'd first hear from Judy, and then Anna's show me the outfits. Afterwards, I'd look at the photos, which were interesting and glamorous, and write about them. Anna wasn't really talkative or wordy, and I never saw her attempt to write anything."

Wheeler recalls Anna teaching him two new things. The first was how to correctly apply mascara. The other was the significance of British artist David Hockney and his critically praised paintings of swimming pools in Southern California. Anna mentioned Hockney to Wheeler since she was utilizing borrowed pools as backgrounds for some location photographs.

Wheeler, like most others at Savvy, saw Anna as "an exotic flower in our midst." Her presence titillated the staff, but they were not in awe of her. Most people, including Wheeler, thought Anna was "very icy, quite British, and extremely upper class." Wheeler was particularly offended by Anna's treatment of Georgia Gunn, whom she viewed as her boss's whipping girl. "That's certainly the impression I had of her," Wheeler says. "Anna merely directed her, and Georgia did as she was told." "She did the heavy lifting, and I don't mean metaphorically, since there were all these clothes that needed to be shifted around," Wheeler admits.

Anna and Wheeler almost fell over each other on Fifty-seventh Street between Fifth and Madison a couple years after they both left Savvy. "I said, 'Hey, Anna,' but she just looked through me and killed me, like she didn't know who I was. It was wonderful." (Wheeler told the experience to one of Anna's young features editors at the magazine in the summer of 2003, many years after Anna had been Vogue's editor in chief. She wasn't astonished. "It happens to individuals she's working with right now, all the time," she revealed.)

Carol Devine Carson, Savvy's highly skilled art director, worked more closely with Anna than the other six or seven full-time personnel, particularly in photo selection and layout. While she admired Anna's fashion sense, she was aware of flaws and quirks.

"She was always gushing about the outfits," Carson recalls, ultimately becoming art director at the publishing giant Knopf. "We did a whole series of items with polka dots, and it was all'staggering' to Anna." . . totally astonishing . . . These kids are incredible.' There was always a little self-promotion in her speeches when she'd deliver her items. It was never what we thought, but what she thought— "Isn't it fabulous?" . . Isn't she stunning? . . 'Aren't these amazing photographs?' Everything was always a little overhyped. Many individuals do this, and I understand why, but it was consistent with her."

Carson gradually grew to believe that some, if not all, of Anna's enthusiasm for the fashion pages she created stemmed from an obsessive desire to be praised. "'You have to make this photo spread seem spectacular,' she'd say. They have to enjoy it. "They've got to adore it," Carson continues, referring to Daniels and Savvy's hard-nosed publisher, Alan Bennett, who held equity in the magazine, played an active role in its style and feel, and was loathed by the majority of the staff, including Daniels.

"They" were most likely referring to editors at rival magazines that keep a close watch on the competition for imaginative fresh talent to hire. After all, Anna saw Savvy as a rest stop, and she knew exactly where she was going. Carson, like the rest of the employees, thought

Anna to be exceedingly ambitious and icy—"not the kind to joke about hairdos and lovers."

Carson subsequently ran into Anna while she was hosting a book party at the St. Regis Hotel. "I said, 'Hello, my name is Carol, and we used to work at Savvy.' I wasn't even on her screen." She didn't say anything to me. She didn't want to be reminded of her time there because Savvy had been a lifeline for her."

While Anna turned off the majority of the female employees at Savvy, she quickly bonded with the one male on board, Dan Taylor, who was seven years younger, good-looking, aristocratic, and dapper, a Southerner hired as Carol Carson's assistant art director and designer because of creative work he had done for IBM and Coca-Cola while working at an Atlanta agency.

Anna brought Taylor to upscale restaurants like The Palm and Mr. Chow's for lunch and dinner, had him house-sit for her, and introduced him to her drugged-out, wild-man companion Rowan Johnson—"a nutcase from hell," Taylor says—the only Viva staffer with whom she stayed close.

Taylor remembers Anna from those days as "young and kickin'." He was nicknamed "the Thin Man" by her because he resembled William Powell and wore fancy pleated slacks like the dashing private dick of 1930s and 1940s cinema.

Anna's involvement in Taylor generated some issues between him and Sara, his future wife, because they had so much fun and hung out together. Taylor was living with Sara, who worked in theater, and Anna was constantly trying to set him up with beautiful ladies.

"Dan had a thing for Anna. . . . He had a [friendly] relationship with her, and he's an exceptional talent, which Anna recognized because she surrounds herself with talented people," Sara Taylor recalls years later. "She frequently presented him to women she thought would be more suitable for him. She exposed him to a lot of high crust people, mostly stylists and French people who were snobbish. "The opportunities were always there."

"I'd rather not go there," Dan Taylor says of Anna interfering in his connection with his future wife.

Taylor felt Anna was beautiful from the moment he met her. She leaned coquettishly against his desk in tight shorts and exposing T-shirts at work. "Oh, Gosh, she was nicely put together," he recalls from those days. At the same time, he saw past her flirtation and realized she was motivated, enterprising, and looking for another job. While her long-term objective was Vogue, she had her sights set on another high-profile publication. Taylor recalls, "She told me she was shooting for New York." "At the moment, it was her aim. She intended to keep working her way up to Vogue. She at least had a budget to work with at Viva. Savvy was merely a blip on the radar. Everyone knew she was on her way somewhere."

Anna worked closely with Taylor after he joined the team, and he described her as "inspiring" as well as "a pain in the ass."

"It was always 'simply' if she didn't like something—a layout, the images."

'A Savvy Choice terrible' was the operative term. . . 'Totally terrible,' was her catchphrase at the time. She was really demanding. She was driven and went through people like toilet paper.

"I was continually clashing with her because she insisted on large covers in magazines to promote herself." She wanted eye-catching things that made her stand out. The happier she was, the better you made her look with the design and layout. Otherwise, she was really dissatisfied. She rapidly became bored if it did not excite her. It required a lot to keep her entertained and moving. She wanted you to accomplish your best, and she'd reject you until you got there. That's a wonderful skill to have."

Taylor, like others who had worked with Anna up to that time, believes Anna's strength was in identifying creative people to carry out her vision. "She has the capacity to hire amazing photographers for us." She was able to get all of these women to pose for her, and it was all done on the spur of the moment because we had no money at Savvy, no budget. Anna was the catalyst, the focal point. She'd get the folks fired up, let them run a little bit, but primarily hold them back until she got what she wanted, getting them to attempt to do something for her on a shoestring."

Yet, due of the harm done on one such low-budget shoot, the magazine's reputation, as well as Anna's, could have suffered.

Taylor, like Anna, believed Guy Le Baube, her fun-loving French shooter, was a jerk, and they occasionally hung out together. Anna utilized Le Baube on several of her Savvy pieces, and he was always spiritedly funny, doing "atrocious things with the models, or anything obscene" to aggravate her, to see her fume and sweat, because he knew how serious, focused, and uptight she was about the job.

All of this was highlighted by an episode that became legendary among a small group of fashion insiders. It took place in Southampton, at an extremely chichi mansion lent to Anna for a day's shoot, with an unusual cast that included Le Baube as photographer and a flamboyant transvestite as Le Baube's assistant and hairdresser. Because the assistant was Muslim, he didn't drink or eat pig, despite Le Baube's best efforts to force them on him in front of Anna, who, he claims, "enjoyed the cruelty of it."

So they were a small party who landed in the sunny Hamptons for the shoot. However, Anna was her normal self, and she wrung a promise from both of them that there would be no monkey business this time. They sincerely swore to conduct themselves professionally.

"We said yes, we'll be good lads," Le Baube chuckles.

Anna should have known better, for despite the fact that she and Le Baube's assistant got along well and she liked the way he cut her hair, he was a troublemaker.

"He liked to torment Anna, and Anna enjoyed being terrorized at times." "So she hired us as two brutes—a horrible heterosexual French photographer and a really faggy, bitchy Muslim queen who was fierce, who loved to get into the models' outfits, put on the high heels, and walk around like a tramp," Le Baube explains. "He was a buddy of mine, yet he sickened me. Anna was naturally devoid of humor since she is extremely efficient, and efficient people do not waste time. We decided to torment her as a joke because she was distressed." But the joke got out of hand.

Anna had given the assistant and Le Baube strong instructions not to disrupt anything in the house, and especially not to damage or break anything, and to return everything moved to its original location. The building was filled with costly art and antiques, and Anna was in charge of the shoot, with her and the magazine's names on the line.

Soon after Le Baube began shooting, the assistant began his schtick: he began to dance, bounce off the walls, and bump into stuff. Anna was stunned as she saw him go completely insane. Suddenly, he dropped to the floor, gripping his chest, stating he thought he was suffering a heart attack, his face distorted in apparent pain. Then he slowly rose to his feet, twisted and turned around the room, colliding with objects, falling into a chair and knocking it over, scratching and destroying the rug and shattering a vase.

"Anna was paralyzed, astounded by what was occurring," Le Baube claims. She was terrified and fled the scene. We were laughing so hard that our stomachs hurt."

The damage was repaired, and Anna was able to keep her employment and reputation. The layout, which featured models by the pool, was titled "A Bigger Splash."

A Territorial Grab

Anna's bossy British demeanor initially irritated several of her American coworkers in New York. They started teasing her, telling her, "Your father is British, your mother is American." Oh, honey, it's like Judaism; you're your mother's religion, so you're an American." Anna, who could dish it out, could typically take it and preserved a stiff upper lip. Nevertheless, to everyone's astonishment, a harmless and fun prank drove her to tears on at least one occasion.

The climate in New York's newsroom was either too hot or too cold, and on a particularly sweltering summer afternoon, Anna yanked her bob off her brow and neck and rubber-banded hair into a topknot. After admiring her new style, one of the office clowns did the same to his hair, and soon everyone in the workplace followed in. Even Ed Kosner emerged from his office, donning his Dunhill jacket and pulling his hair up.

Anna, who was accustomed to ignoring everyone around her, had no idea what was going on. "But when she got up from her desk to take a trip around the office, she was astonished to see everybody with their hair up precisely like her," Jordan Schaps, one of the few colleagues with whom she had bonded, says. "When she realized she was being humiliated, she fell into tears and left the office for the day." Her English sensibility, I assume, didn't like being the butt of that kind of humour. She didn't laugh or understand the joke."

There were attempts to integrate Anna into the New York family, such as invites to staff social occasions, one of which was a traditional New England clambake. Anna was stunned when she received the invitation. "What exactly is a clambake?" " she inquired of a coworker. She was informed it's a lot of fun—lobster, clams, corn, beer, and everyone has a fantastic time on the beach.

"Everyone was dressed in old jeans, shorts, and T-shirts, and Anna came in wrapped in a whole Issye Miyake white, pleated three-piece costume, with the stiletto shoes," a coworker recalls, still chuckling about the occasion years later. "I told Anna, 'You know, we're going to sit on the beach,' but she didn't have to. The guys all stood up and spread blankets and jackets for her, and while everyone else was eating with their hands, Anna was eating with utensils. Even at a clambake, she could always run the show."

One of the keys to Anna's success was her ability to hire innovative photographers, most of whom were guys, and have them work hard to make her seem attractive. "What she did so well was she never pretended to be delighted with their work," a former New York editor observes, "so these men were always jumping through hoops and performing backflips for her." And the way she kept them doing it was to let them know they weren't quite up to par."

Anna was always looking for new creative shooters to add to her roster, so when Andrea Blanche called to say she had a narrative idea, she immediately scheduled a meeting for drinks. Blanche had never heard of Anna until she saw a few of her layouts in New York and thought they were quite stylish. Blanche, a "idea person," thought her notion would be a good fit for the type of job Anna was doing. "I found her to be extremely open to meeting with me," she says. "My reputation was established, she knew of me, and that's why she answered the phone and agreed to meet."

While Blanche was a female photographer, she was significant to Anna because she worked for Vogue and was a favorite of Alex Liberman. Anna would not have made time for anyone else.

They met for about a half hour at a restaurant, where Blanche offered her "journalistic fashion notion," which she thought would fit in with what New York was doing. Anna sat and listened intently, reclining back in her chair, hands on the table, without touching her wine or taking notes. Blanche, who is gregarious, noticed Anna's lack of reaction, being "reserved," and appearing "aloof," and when Blanche was finished, Anna responded. "She told me right away that she didn't like the idea and that it wasn't something she could use or was suitable for the magazine."

Blanche was naturally "disappointed" and "surprised," because she normally had a solid sense of what editors liked. "I always try to tailor the piece to the editor, and I thought this would work for her."

Blanche thanked Anna for her time before the two parted ways.

Blanche was flipping through the current issue of New York when she froze. The story concept she had offered and Anna had rejected was staring back at her, photographed by a male photographer.

Blanche was stunned, and the thoughts racing through her mind concerning Anna at the time were, as she recounts years later, "not very positive things!" I believe you are always astonished when you believe someone has stolen something from you and stolen your concept. After all, my ideas are how I make a living, so it's difficult to take when you know someone's stolen from you." Blanche says the politics at Vogue at the time allowed such things to happen, and that one had to adapt to continue in the game. "But Anna was a newcomer to New York. new venue, so I took her word for it. When I read my piece in the magazine, I was furious and probably yelled some expletives."

Oliviero Toscani was another well-known photographer with whom Anna clashed, but this time she bore the brunt of the vitriol. Anna was working on a project with Jordan Schaps, who was taken aback by the scene. Toscani had come late from Paris and was exhausted from the journey. But Anna, who was working on a tight timetable, needed to get started right away.

"We were like acolytes waiting for him because he was a wonderful, brilliant man, but instead of being kind, he was devastatingly harsh to Anna," Schaps adds. "He didn't care about the clothes, didn't care about the girls, and was just a brute, a sarcastic brute." He strutted around like an angry peacock, criticizing everything Anna had laid out, and he was so cruel that he brought Anna to tears. "I was astounded by his actions and astounded by her sensitivity."

Toscani loved Anna's taste and originality, but he refused to be frightened by her, unlike other photographers. "If Anna tried to pull any of her nonsense with him, it wouldn't work," a coworker observes. He didn't need her permission. She required his assistance. That's why he could make her cry, and why he presumably did it—to remind her of that."

Not everything with Anna was always so psychologically challenging, especially when she was working with fun-loving photographers like Guy Le Baube, who triggered a panic episode in the start of one of Anna's first large fashion shoots for New York. The story was titled "Heat of the Night," and it starred Andie MacDowell, a lovely young model from North Carolina who went on to become an actor and cosmetics ambassador.

The location was a narrow ledge after dark outside Dianne B. Le Baube's midtown Manhattan penthouse office. Le Baube, who had been given mostly free rein by Anna because his work was valuable, had decided he wanted MacDowell in the foreground, with the Empire State Building in the background, but on a slant and not level with his camera.

This was before computer software could cheat anything like that, so Le Baube decided to jerry-rig a platform with side rails and extend it out the window, thirty storeys above the street, and angle it. Anna had obtained a classic chair from the Museum of Modern Art, which would be put on the platform and in which MacDowell would be photographed. It was a risky setup.

The only thing Anna objected to was Le Baube's suggestion that a floor fan blow up the pantyless MacDowell's fancy gown. He reasoned that it would keep her cool while also giving the dress the appearance of a billowing sail, with the Empire State Building suggesting a sailboat straining against the wind. However, Anna felt that the altitude where they were working was dangerously windy enough, and that MacDowell "didn't need a breeze between her legs."

The shoot went smoothly, and the images turned out nicely. But, by the end of the hour-long shoot, Andie MacDowell's physical and emotional state had changed.

"Andie has incredibly gorgeous eyes but terrible eyesight," Le Baube explains. "It wasn't until we were done shooting that she realized she was two feet from the edge on the thirty-first floor with no pants on—and she had vertigo." She became disoriented and afraid, began crying, and yelled that she didn't want to be there. What was amusing was that Andie is partially blind, and she had no idea we had put her in such a precarious predicament. She screamed when she realized what had happened.

"The beauty of it was that Anna handled it so wonderfully." "I've always liked to explore, and Anna let me do just that," he says. "I could have had Andie MacDowell walk on a thread between two skyscrapers and Anna would not have batted an eyelid." She was just interested in the photographs."

Anna, more aggressive, ambitious, and confident than ever, saw a chance to broaden her power base in New York beyond fashion. She was initially in charge of the special spring and fall fashion issues, but she later expanded into furniture design, personality pieces, and other aspects of style. "She took over design and food issues," a former editor adds. "She persuaded Kosner to give her everything." He gave her everything she desired."

Anna realized she could make a territorial grab without stomping on too many toes. She discovered there was a style vacuum at the magazine that only she could fill after attentively studying the terrain and perceiving it in a new light. Because her talent was all visual, she had Kosner's ear and imposed direction, suggesting concepts no one else on staff had ever dreamt of, let alone produced. So she pushed forth, just like any adventurous, ambitious, and motivated man in the same situation and with the same foresight.

"She branched out and made up for the rest of us' lack of imagination," says Nancy McKeon, who was writing all of Anna's material. "At the same time, she took herself seriously in a pretty frivolous business because her actual project and commodity was herself."

"She wanted to clean up New York magazine and add a touch of style, so she devised this rotation—a page of home furnishings one week, a page of fashion the next, a page of girl-around-town celebrity something or other the next—and this rotation brought a whole new level of photography and style thinking to New York that was very positive." Yet everything she did instilled resentment in everyone."

It was a perfect time for Anna to be working as a fashion editor in New York, a time when "artists, fashion designers, and interior decorators were in fierce competition with each other for celebrity status," as she later described it. She explained her thoughts to Kosner, who gave her permission to take advantage of the situation—"to break away from the usual catalog formula of fashion journalism."

Yet, several of the elements Anna proposed were completely irrelevant, leaving McKeon and other staffers perplexed.

Clio Goldsmith, a minor British actress, was the subject of one girl-around-town narrative. In the early 1980s, Goldsmith appeared in several French and Italian B movies that aired on late-night TV. Anna opted to showcase her in New York at that time for no clear reason other than she was appearing in another stupid sex farce called Le Cadeau (The Gift) and was going to spend some time in Manhattan.

Anna, for whatever reason, asked McKeon to create some text blocks to accompany images of Goldsmith. For once, the wordsmith was stumped; she couldn't figure out what to do because Anna had given her no additional information or direction. Furthermore, She couldn't see why anything about this unknown actress should be published other than the fact that one Brit was seemingly marketing another, so she approached Kosner and asked, "What the heck is this?" What are we doing? What can I do in this situation? "

"Well, it's interesting," Kosner said lamely. Do it for Anna." And that was the end of it.

Kosner and his wife, Julie Baumgold, a contributing writer for New York at the time, had "social ambitions" and saw Anna as a blazing star in their glittering Manhattan constellation, according to McKeon and others. "Kosner saw Anna transforming a section of New York into a fashion, trend-setting magazine, which I assume he believed would work well for him and Julie on the cocktail circuit," a colleague observes.

Kosner, like so many other guys, was caught and entranced by Anna, who knew how to use it and read him. "She figured here's this guy who has this sort of idea of himself, who's social, who always mentions buying his clothes at Paul Stuart," McKeon said. "Anna was really sexy in an all-girl type of way." She was having a Japanese phase, so she wore these dresses loose and without a bra, and she had a juicy body—very skinny, but not the anorexic thing she's done afterwards where she's all head. She always applied perfume before going in to see Ed. So she had a strong sense that she was a weapon, that she herself was a power."

Another editor recalls Anna walking into Kosner's office "in high heels, elegantly dressed, batting her enormous eyes and saying to him, 'I know you'll agree with this.'" . and acquire whatever she desired.``

Anna's work, such as the time she commissioned a collection of well-known artists to create backdrops with models in the foreground, left Kosner speechless. "It was a fantastic piece for us and a real first at the time," he added later. "It's become such a standard today, but Anna was absolutely the first." Anna had made numerous social contacts in the art world, including flashy New York gallery owner Mary Boone, who represented painters like David Salle and Julian Schnabel, who took part in the model background shoot. (Anna may have gotten the idea from set designers on Cathy McGowan's Ready, Steady, Go! dance show when she was a teenager in London.)

While Kosner granted Anna free reign to do whatever she wanted within her expanding realm, several of the female colleagues, like "Best Bets" Corky Pollan, who co-wrote blurbs with McKeon about things to buy, see, and do in the city, developed a territorial anxiety. Pollan feared the worst for Anna and acted as a modern-day Paul Revere, warning the villagers of an impending British onslaught. And her apprehension was justified. Anna loathed "Best Picks," seeing it as a collection of dull images with uninteresting suggestions, so she gained Kosner's ear and began dummying up well-orchestrated still lifes, such as a layout with everything white. "The woman's ego was out of control," McKeon adds. Sensing that a revolution was brewing in the newsroom, Pollan kept a watchful eye on the enemy from her "Best Bets' ' desk, which was near to Anna's white Formica command position.

"Corky came to me one day and said, 'We'd best watch our backs,'" McKeon recounts, "and I asked her what she meant, and she said, 'Oh, if we don't look out, this woman's going to take over everything.'" She's going to take all of our jobs.' Two weeks later,

Anna's one-page fashion, home furnishings, and celebrity profiles began to appear. "Yet, 'Best Bets' remained."

One of those shots included a segment shot in a Hamptons house Anna had rented. The cover image Anna was striving for was of a woman with a highly costly piece of cowhide draped over her in a sophisticated manner. Working on the shoot with her was Jordan Schaps, who had some reservations about Anna's vision and finally felt obligated to speak his opinion. "Do you really think the New York magazine woman is going to go out and spend $5,000 on a leather hide to fling around?" he asked Anna. " Anna locked her gaze on him for a few moments before declaring, " 'My love, I don't mind if they go to Woolworth's and buy a lump of cloth. It's not about fashion, it's about style,' she replied, and I was quite pleased by her attitude."

Under Kosner, three cardinal sins might result in an employee's dismissal: lying on an expense report, leaking internal information about a story, and granting a subject copy or photo approval. Anna committed the third offense. Anybody else would have been fired on the spot, but Kosner broke the rules because the violation was Anna.

Anna approached another editor who worked on the article after completing a summer styles shoot with the seductive new actress Rachel Ward and sought the final layout photographs, stating she wanted to give them to Ward for her approval—an absolute no-no, which Anna knew.

While reviewing the model release form, the editor was in for an even bigger surprise. Anna had actually granted Ward, who wasn't a big star at the time, consent over the images in writing. Bottom line: If the Australian-born actress didn't like the photos and refused to accept them, the story might die. "Maybe Anna didn't expect Ward to hold us to it. "Maybe Anna thought she could get away with it," the associate speculated years later.

Even back then, long before celebrities became a mainstay of every type of magazine from sports to fashion, Anna predicted that attractive stars like Ward on the cover would sell copies, and she was desperate to land one at any cost.

The editor informed Kosner of the serious situation, and he invited Anna for a secret meeting. "Ed was not pleased," a worker recalls, and the next morning Anna was on a plane to La-La Land—on her own dime—with the images in hand, hoping to gain the subject's permission. In order to save the tale, Kosner presumably gave Anna permission to break the no-show rule.

Anna, for whatever reason, wanted McKeon to produce some text blocks to accompany photographs of Goldsmith. For once, the wordsmith was perplexed; she couldn't figure out what to do because Anna had provided no extra information or direction. Additionally, she couldn't understand why anything about this unknown actress should be publicized other than the fact that one Brit was apparently marketing another, so she approached Kosner and asked, "What the heck is this?" What can I do in this situation? "

"Oh, it's intriguing," Kosner mumbled. Do it for Anna." And that was the end of it.

According to McKeon and others, Kosner and his wife, Julie

Baumgold, who was a contributing writer for New York at the time, had "social ambitions" and saw Anna as a blazing star in their glittering Manhattan constellation. "Kosner saw Anna transforming a section of New York into a fashion, trend-setting magazine, which I assume he believed would work well for him and Julie on the cocktail circuit," a colleague observes.

"She figured here's this guy who has this sort of idea of himself, who's social, who always mentions buying his clothes at Paul Stuart," McKeon said. "Anna was really sexy in an all-girl type of way." She was having a Japanese phase, so she wore these dresses loose and without a bra, and she had a juicy body—very skinny, but not the anorexic thing she's done since.

Another editor recalls Anna arriving into Kosner's office "in high heels, finely dressed, batting her large eyes and saying to him, 'I know you'll agree with this.'" and obtain everything she desired.``

Anna's work, such as the time she commissioned a group of well-known artists to create backdrops with models in the foreground, left Kosner speechless. "It was a fantastic piece for us and a real first at the time," he later added. "It's become such a standard today, but Anna was absolutely the first."

While Kosner gave Anna free rein to do whatever she wanted within her expanding realm, several female colleagues, such as "Best Bets" Corky Pollan, who co-wrote blurbs with McKeon about things to buy, see, and do in the city, developed territorial anxiety. Pollan feared the worst for Anna and acted as a modern-day Paul Revere, warning the villagers of an impending British onslaught.

"Corky came to me one day and said, 'We'd better watch our backs,'" McKeon recalls, "and I asked her what she meant, and she said, 'Oh, if we don't look out, this woman's going to take over everything.'" Two weeks later, Anna's one-page fashion, home furnishings, and celebrity profiles began to appear. "Yet, 'Best Bets' remained."

One of those shots included a segment shot in a Hamptons house Anna had rented. The cover image Anna was aiming for was of a woman with a highly expensive piece of cowhide draped over her in a sophisticated manner. Working on the shoot with her was Jordan Schaps, who had some reservations about Anna's vision and finally felt obligated to speak his opinion.

" he asked Anna. " Anna locked her gaze on him for a few moments before proclaiming, " 'My love, I don't mind if people go to Woolworth's and purchase a lump of material. It's not about fashion, it's about style,' she replied, and I was rather delighted by her attitude."

According to Kosner, three cardinal sins may result in an employee's dismissal: lying on an expense report, leaking internal information about a story, and providing subject copy or photo approval. Anna committed the third infraction. Anybody else would have been dismissed on the instant, but Kosner broke the rules because the transgression was Minor.

Anna approached another editor who worked on the piece after completing a summer styles shoot with the attractive new actress Rachel Ward and requested the final layout images, claiming she wanted to give them to Ward for her approval—an absolute no-no, which Anna knew.

The editor was in for an even larger surprise while perusing the model release form. Anna had actually provided Ward, who wasn't a famous figure at the time, written permission to use the photographs. Bottom line: If the Australian-born actress didn't like the images and refused to accept them, the tale might die. "Maybe Anna didn't expect Ward to hold us to it. "Perhaps Anna thought she could get away with it," the associate speculated years later.

Even back then, long before celebrities became a staple of every sort of magazine from sports to fashion, Anna prophesied that gorgeous stars like Ward on the cover would sell copies, and she was desperate to land one at any cost.

"Ed was not pleased," a worker recalls, and the next morning Anna was on a jet to La-La Land—on her own dime—with the photographs in hand, hoping to gain the subject's approval. In order to rescue the tale, Kosner probably gave Anna permission to break the no-show rule.

As Anna's aide de camp, this intriguing new figure was introduced into the Vogue battles.

Blow felt an instant connection with Anna. "Like me, she was obsessed with fashion." If you look at her, you'll notice that she surrounds herself with obsessive people like André Leon Talley, who are all completely obsessed with fashion."

Blow claims that most of her work for Anna consisted of "very uninteresting tasks" like delivering her shoes to the cobbler to be reheeled, and that she was "quite intimidated" by Anna's "organization and iron determination." As a phone call came through, Anna saved the message in a folder. "Everything would be filed, every discussion would be filed, every single piece of paper." To avoid being chastised by Anna for being sloppy, Blow began wiping her own desk with Perrier at the end of the day.

She also noticed how much Anna relied on her husband for moral support during her nine-month spell. "David used to mentor her," she explains. "I don't believe she could have done it without him." David was an excellent tactician. He was logical and exact. He thought more clearly since he was a psychiatrist. She was always on the phone with him. He'd know how to deal with people as a psychiatrist."

The bottom line, though, was that Anna was "an inspiration." I admired her."

"Anna liked Blow because she was a character," Schechter explains. Issy reminded me of a weird, eccentric British bird. She'd show up to work with the tiniest of skirts and fishnet hose with rips, probably not on purpose, but because she tripped and ripped them, and her lipstick was always off the side of her mouth."

Blow's style began to disrupt the smooth operation of the creative director's office, sparking a battle inside a conflict. Schechter found herself working twice as hard to ensure that Blow, who spent a lot of time on the phone with pals, was functioning well. Other, more significant problems developed, such as when Blow "lost a photographer's portfolio" and "threatened to sue for a hundred thousand dollars," according to Schechter. Schechter dropped ten pounds when she initially started working for Anna at Vogue because she went up and down thirteen flights of stairs to do errands rather than wasting time waiting for elevators. With Blow on board, "I was on the verge of a nervous collapse." Everyone admired Dizzy Issy—"Isn't she funny?" 'Look at her ripped stockings.' But she was hostile toward me."

She couldn't handle it any longer and complained to Anna. "I had to go to her because she was about to lose me—not because I was going to quit, but because I was going to collapse."

Blow had linked with Anna's protégé, André Leon Talley, who "adored" her and saw her as an eccentric muse, and invited her to work as his assistant. "She and André weren't talking after three months," Schechter adds, and she departed.

Blow returned to England and tried unsuccessfully to freelance for Vogue, but quickly discovered that "Anna's a terrific one for rejecting pieces." If I'm not mistaken, she's famous for it. She's a stickler for detail."

By 2004, Blow had established herself as a celebrity in her own right in England. She had worked as a fashion stylist for British Vogue and was now the fashion director of the London Sunday Times and Tatler, where she kept a rack of her own apparel in addition to her forty-thousand-dollar custom-built wardrobe at home. She has been credited with discovering designers such as Alexander McQueen and Philip Treacy over the years.

"Anna always invites me to the American Vogue parties when I go to the shows." She was always proud of me while I worked for her. They nickname her the ice maiden, but I don't believe she is one. "I imagine her to be like the Concorde, floating into the clouds."

Marriage Made in Heaven

Anna and David Shaffer had a fast courtship, and he proposed right away, but she declined to respond right away. She kept the expensive ring he gave her but never wore it. It wasn't until a few months later, in early 1984, that he got the answer he was looking for, but in the most unusual way.

Shaffer had accompanied Anna to the Paris collections, the same trip that sparked the brawl with Jade Hobson and Polly Mellen. During their trip, she met her father for drinks at the elegant Ritz Hotel's bar. Anna communicated with Charles Wintour relatively infrequently at the time for a variety of reasons. Aside from being completely consumed by her career in New York, she was still enraged by his marriage to Audrey Slaughter and his treatment of her mother.

Win-tour observed a "really nice" diamond on Anna's left hand's fourth finger as the father and daughter shared a rare private time over drinks. When he questioned what it was, she disclosed it was her engagement ring, and Shaffer was the fortunate recipient.

Although Wintour was aware that Anna and Shaffer were deeply attached, and regarded the therapist as "an absolute saint" for looking after her professional and personal interests, he had no idea their relationship had progressed to the point of marriage. He was overjoyed.

When Wintour was admiring Anna's ring, Shaffer appeared at the bar, and his future father-in-law congratulated him. Shaffer appeared "somewhat shocked," unsure of what was going on. Then Anna carefully raised her hand, and Shaffer noticed that she'd finally put on the sparkler, which surprised both him and her father.

Anna had informed Shaffer when he originally proposed that she would put on the ring only when she was absolutely ready to marry him, not earlier. She chose that unromantic moment at the Ritz bar with her father by her side to tell Shaffer she was now saying yes.

"David usually tells Anna that was the evening I proposed to him," Charles Wintour later revealed.

The peculiar manner in which Anna handled it all revealed something about the complexities of her connection with the guy who would become her husband, as well as which partner was ultimately in charge of their relationship. According to many who know her, Anna is "the ultimate control freak" in both her professional and personal lives. It also expressed her thoughts regarding her father's remarriage and how essential his approval was to her at all times. How many women tell their father they've accepted a marriage proposal before telling their future husband? Anna, on the other hand, placed a high value on her father's acceptance of her future spouse. While many in Anna's circle thought Shaffer was an unusual choice, he was most likely the first man in Anna's life whom Charles Wintour actually approved of—and Anna had always been a daddy's girl who desired his favor.

Returning to New York, Anna re-entered the Vogue wars, and she and Shaffer, who had yet to pick a wedding date, began supervising the repair of a four-story mid-nineteenth-century brownstone in Greenwich Village. The house, with its maze of little rooms, had been abandoned for years and was in disrepair, but Anna saw it as her dream home.

She enlisted the help of a friend, high-tech New York architect and designer Alan Buchsbaum, to creatively preserve the house's original details while still making it modernistic and unique.

Anna met Buchsbaum while working at New York magazine. He and a few other well-known interior designers had been chosen by her to do various rooms for a dramatic and unique layout. Buchsbaum was a celebrity architect who had worked with Christie Brinkley, Bette Midler, Diane Keaton, and Ellen Barkin, among others. But he and Anna had a unique bond, and they frequently socialized, ate dinner together, gossiped, and discussed fashion. He was one of many gay guys in her acquaintance, owing to her involvement in the fashion business. Buchsbaum, like Anna, was reticent, yet he lit up once he saw her. Unfortunately, he was one of the first American victims of AIDS in her life, dying at the age of 51 in 1987. Following his death, Anna made the sickness one of her causes by hosting a fund-raising fashion show in New York called Seventh on Sale.

Anna oversaw the entire house renovation show, according to Davis Sprinkle, Buchsbaum's business associate. "She actually had some pretty specific thoughts about the inner feeling," Sprinkle recalls years later. "David was unquestionably less involved in the overall project." He clearly let her make the decisions. She was in charge of the majority of the process. If she didn't like something, she'd let me know." Was she tough to deal with? "We forget the negative stuff with time," he says.

Anna had a fixation for neatness and stark minimalism, thus walls were pulled down, and at least one room, the dining room, featured a pair of columns instead of a door marking the entrance. "Working at a magazine is a never-ending feast for the eyes; you spend your days gazing at stuff," she once commented about the remodeling. "As a result, I prefer a more tranquil environment at home."

Along with the house, Buchsbaum designed a high-tech and elegant power desk for Anna, which was later marketed as the "Wintour Table" by the French firm Ecart International. Its wooden frame and legs, set on the diagonal, were made of ebonized mahogany, and its top was a lacquered sheet of cold steel. Anna treasured her desk above all else and had it sent across the Atlantic twice: once when she took over British Vogue and again when she returned to become editor in chief of Home & Garden and then American Vogue.

The desk, like her haircut and sunglasses, became a part of Wintour's signature, and she was still overseeing things from behind it in 2004, in her second decade as editor-in-chief of Vogue. She describes it as "extremely clean," "a bit quirky," and "with a sense of humor." It lacks drawers because she prefers to have "everything out in the open," and she appreciates its narrowness because "I don't want people to feel far away while they're talking to me." . . (Since Anna's desk resembled a table, everyone could see through the bottom. "It was funny," Laurie Schechter recalls, "because Anna sat behind her desk like a man, with her knees spread...

While the property was being renovated, Anna and Shaffer rented a loft with Hudson River views in the far West Village, near the West Side Highway. Anna's flat, which allowed her to witness the QE2 arrive and depart, was in a foreboding structure that used to be a jail. The loft's owner was a British woman named Charlotte Noel, who had been in Anna's little circle when she first moved to New York a decade before. Noel was leaving the neighborhood and moving uptown, so Anna and Shaffer opted to rent her property because it was close to their townhouse renovation and acquaintances in the neighborhood.

"When they rented from me, it was an ordinary loft with very little furniture and not very comfortable, and the neighborhood was really dismal, pretty unattractive, and quite bleak," she explains. "Dead bodies were being fished out of the river, the Mafia had complete control over all waste trucks, and there were all those gay S&M clubs." It was pretty rough," but Anna and Shaffer didn't mind because they thought it was a cool environment and took the place after a brief rent discussion.

"Anna was very harsh, very businesslike, and David was rather pitiful, asking things like, 'Could I go and get the sofas covered?'"

Noel recalls. "What I mean is that Anna did nothing, therefore he was left to undertake a lot of what you'd think of as womanly things." It was an unusual connection, and I always thought it was an unusual pairing. They didn't appear to be compatible, either physically or intellectually."

Others were of the opinion that the editor and the psychiatrist were in love and were good for one other. Shaffer had intelligence and was a

82

nice father figure, whereas Anna was cool, beautiful, and younger, someone who boosted the shrink's ego and gave him panache. "Anna desired children. "She desired stability," a friend observes.

Anna and Shaffer, then chief of the juvenile psychiatry department at Columbia Presbyterian Medical Center and the New York State Psychiatric Institute, married on September 7, 1984, in their town residence on MacDougal Street, in a ceremony officiated by New York Civil Court Judge Elliott Wilk. Anna's 35th birthday was coming up in two months. Shaffer was 48 years old. The tiny announcement in the next day's New York Times, most likely the first time Anna had ever been mentioned in the publication, stated that she would keep her last name. Just Harpers & Queen and New York magazine were cited in her previous job history, presumably based on information she had submitted.

Apart from the personalized invitations, the wedding was described by one guest as "a very beautiful, very simple, very quiet intimate family wedding—quite civil, not splashy."

Following the ceremony, Anna's divorced parents, her father's new bride, Anna's siblings, and work friends such as Ed Kosner, Jean Pagliuso and her husband, Laurie Schechter, and Georgia Gunn proceeded to the living-room area, where a large table was set up for a joyful lunch.

Charles Wintour stood at the table and proposed a toast to his favorite child and her groom. He reminded the audience that Anna was now living her ambition of becoming an editor at Vogue. "My father is extremely kind in a subtle kind of way," Anna said years later. He mentioned each of David's two children at length in his speech at my wedding to show them they were a vital part of the family." (The two teenage boys from Shaffer's former marriage would live with the newlyweds.)

"It was a great wedding," Schechter says. "They had made their own vows." It looked like a wonderful match to me."

Others, such as Anna's coworker and friend Paul Sinclaire, were startled that they had married. "I would have bet that the wedding would not have happened, and if it had, their marriage would have lasted a year and a half, let alone having two kids," he adds, reflecting on the affair that ended the marriage years later. "I believe she married David because he was so intelligent." He was never a beauty."

Anna fell pregnant roughly seven months after the wedding, in April 1985.

The same month, in London, an event occurred that would have far-reaching consequences for her future. Beatrix Miller announced her departure from British Vogue after twenty-one years at the head, stating that she was departing to write novels. Miller, like Anna, was a tough cookie and a taskmaster. "You have exactly two minutes," she would say gruffly to a potential employee. "Tell me about yourself," she once told a group of four dozen colleagues. "I want

you all know that, as far as I'm concerned, the July issue is a write-off. There is a mistake on page 136," she said. The workforce was now contemplating their future as reports began to circulate over the water that a nuclear blast in the slim form of Anna Wintour was on its way to them. Condé Nast's top executives, Si Newhouse and Alex Liberman, remained tight-lipped about Miller's replacement.

Meanwhile, the pregnant Anna was busy pushing her way to the front of the book at Vogue and becoming Shaffer's stepmother.

Friends of Shaffer's ex-wife, as well as Anna and David Shaffer, speculate that the psychiatrist "must have applied his own brand of psychology to the kids" because they turned out so well. "The boys were always exceptional and precocious in the finest manner, and they always seemed connected to their parents," Dianne Benson explains.

The lower level of the couple's exquisite town house was occupied by Shaffer's sons, who were simply outfitted with basic but elegant English and American antique pieces—a Federal sofa, a Queen Anne tallboy, Empire chairs, tons of books, bare wood flooring, and area rugs. Anna lived the life that Vogue symbolized, and she was a gold bullion asset, which drew Alex Liberman and, eventually, Si Newhouse to her.

The upper level of the house had been turned into the couple's huge master bedroom suite, which was modestly furnished with a bed covered in a plain white down blanket, two Victorian slipper chairs, a Queen Anne bureau, an English oak chest, and Anna's collection of little ivory things. The bathroom was big—British-style, like Anna was used to—and featured a fireplace, an old porcelain tub, a marble sink, an English-made large wood-framed mirror, and a nineteenth-century wicker chair.

Anna had chosen that every space needed to be light, open, and uncluttered; she didn't want a Victorian mash-up, which she thought "looked ludicrous when re-created in New York apartments." . . . Nobody does it better than the Brits when it's authentic," she claimed in The New York Times Sunday Magazine, which regarded the magnificent mansion and its powerful Vogue creative director now worthy of her first large spread in 1986.

When it came to Americans and their level of taste, Anna stated they were overly brand-name and designer focused, which was an odd assertion coming from an editor at a magazine that marketed and derived its authority and revenue from designer and brand names. Yet, she believed that the Yanks (presumably the wealthy ones) were unduly preoccupied with "buying Biedermeier this or Josef Hoffman that," and that "designed mansions" bored her to tears. She mentioned that some of her neighbors didn't "get" her house's makeover. They "looked around very bewildered and said, 'I guess this is what you call a loft house,'" she said when invited to visit her home.

Returning at the office, Anna had delegated more responsibilities to Laurie Schechter, such as coordinating photographers, venues, and other details for the book's non fashion section, which Anna now despisedly had to handle alongside Amy Gross at Liberman's request. With the promotion of Schechter, Anna declared that she would engage a secretary/editorial assistant to handle the day-to-day regular work. For almost a minute, Schechter felt relieved.

The new girl's name was Hon. Isabella Delves Broughton Blow is known to her friends as Issy (pronounced Izzy). She was a busty, voluptuous, beet-red-lipped, micro mini skirted eccentric Brit with a braying laugh from Mother England. Jock Delves Broughton, the principal figure in the factual book and film White Mischief, was her grandfather. During WWII, in Kenya, the envious Broughton fatally shot a playboy named Lloyd Erroll, who was having an affair with his attractive and much younger wife, Lady Diana Broughton (played by Greta Scacchi in the 1988 film). Issy's grandma was Lady Diana.

Baby Makes Three

Anna didn't tell her friends or Vogue colleagues—the few with whom she communicated—that she was expecting a child, and most couldn't tell she was pregnant because she remained slender and perfect-looking.

When one of her coworkers found out she was pregnant, she asked Anna how she managed to be so calm. What was Anna's reaction? "Willpower."

Instead of boring, unchic maternity clothes, she merely opened the back of her short, tight Chanel skirt a little to make room for her tummy, and she always wore the suit jacket to work, which helped to conceal her fragile condition. She didn't wear comfy shoes either; she walked around in her stilettos. She was as vivacious as ever. "It wasn't like she was racing out to throw up," Laurie Schechter, her number one lady-in-waiting, observed. She breezed through it."

Her father was one of the few people who knew about her secret from the beginning. The wife of a British journalist who was taught by Charles Wintour at the Evening Standard recalls running into him at the BBC one day, and he was beaming. "When she asked how he was, he was beyond delighted. 'My daughter Anna is going to have a baby, and if it's a boy, she's going to name him Charlie after me,' he exclaimed.

When Anna finally began to reveal to a few female colleagues that she was "up the duff," as they say in England, a number of them were taken aback, mainly because they couldn't imagine the formidable ice queen taking time away from her career to raise a child, let alone holding a baby to her breast and being nurturing, warm, and loving. Yes, Anna Wintour is a motivated editor; nay,

Anna Wintour is a mother. Some thought it was an oxymoron.

"I found it uncomfortable to view her as a mother," photographer Andrea Blanche explains. "I just never saw her in that light." You know, those attributes that I associate with parenthood. "I just never imagined Anna like that," says photographer Jean Pagliuso, who was in the elevator with Anna after a meeting at Vogue and "she just sort of dropped it as an aside." "She didn't want anyone to know she was pregnant at the moment." She seemed happier than I would have expected from Anna."

Along with a grandson, "Chilly Charlie" Wintour was expecting his favorite offspring, a chip off the old block, back in Britain.

In the summer of 1985, rumors began to circulate in the British press that Anna was the main contender for Beatrix Miller's post as editor in chief of British Vogue, and that Anna had spent a week in London being courted but had turned down the offer. She told the Daily Mail's Nigel Dempster that she wasn't taking the job because her husband had accepted a research project on teen suicide, his specialization, and couldn't leave New York without him, and she wasn't traveling without him. "I'd love to work in London and have a British child, but he can't leave," she remarked flatly.

Condé Nast managing director Bernard Leser verified the allegations a few weeks later, on September 18, 1985. It had been agreed, after top-secret plotting and planning, and withholding information from the public, that Anna would indeed become the next editor of British Vogue.

Unbeknownst to most, Anna had been privy to some of the secret meetings and wasn't pleased with the outcome. She had lobbied hard and believed she deserved to succeed Grace Mirabella now rather than later. But, Newhouse and Liberman persuaded her that the time would come. She even used the mom card, complaining about the prospect of a transatlantic marriage. Yet none of it was accepted by the suits. She was forced to play corporate ball.

When asked why the appointment had taken so long, Leser did a rapid two-step in making the public announcement. "American Vogue did not like the notion of losing her," he remarked, which was good for the press and the public to hear.

Yet for those who worked with Anna at American Vogue, the sooner she went, the better. There was no sadness, only joy. Her advancement was both a dream come true and the conclusion of a nightmare. Her many detractors, particularly Mirabella, would be free of her.

Anna's new role was mentioned briefly in Women's Wear Daily, but the British press was buzzing with excitement about the shift in command. The Times proclaimed Miller a "hard act to follow," speculating (wrongly) that Anna "may be expected to stay a decade and demonstrate the glitter and eccentricity that have distinguished Vogue editors since 1916."

One of them went on to head a design house and then spent the rest of her life in bed, another wore purple all the time, and one was a Communist.

The quirkiness of Vogue's ancestors would come to an end with Anna's rule. It was now all business.

"In New York, they regard her as chilly," reported The Guardian, where Anna's brother Patrick became a political correspondent. . . Wintour's iron determination, cool single-mindedness, and achievement define her. . . the outward look of things."

According to the London Times, an unnamed Wintour colleague hailed her as "elegance personified." . . The Times described Liberman as the "grand panjandrum of the international Vogues," saying he gave Anna "a little extra polish" when he appointed her creative director and "instructed her to 'use her elbows.' A minister without portfolio, she seized the situation and rather quickly became the jewel in the Condé Nast crown."

Anna, five months pregnant, pretended to be overjoyed, but the job—the flagship Vogue in New York—was still out of reach. According to Schechter, Anna saw London as an opportunity to become the editor in chief of another Vogue, but she was uninterested. "But, you never see Anna get enthusiastic." She was never the type to leap up and down and express her joy."

Mirabella and her court were ecstatically dancing in the corridors, if Anna wasn't overjoyed with the position. Literally. "I was home sick the day they made the announcement," Jade Hobson recalls. "When my colleague Liz Tretter told me, I could clearly hear hoots and hollers on the floor." That was complete chaos. Several people, including me, were relieved she was leaving."

The decision to ship Anna to London came as a relief to Mirabella. The editor in chief had had enough of the creative director's aggressive and insensitive attempts to fire her. Mirabella had been bombarded with reports that she was about to be fired and replaced with Anna. Since Anna's arrival two years ago, the chatter had spread like wildfire, from the mailroom clerk on up. Outside of Vogue, the lunchtime fashionistas mused about nothing else—Grace was out, and Anna would be in any day now. The whispers spread from the exquisite avenues of Madison, Park, and Fifth to Paris' trendy Avenue Montaigne and Milan's chic Via della Spiga. The fashion and general press also had a field day speculating, chasing anonymous and sometimes well-placed insider suggestions that an announcement about Anna's hiring will be made any day.

Yet Mirabella had taught herself to disregard the supposition or she'd go insane.

Liberman, who loved to incite, manipulate, and provoke, knew how Mirabella felt, and although he told Anna one thing, he told Mirabella another—comforting her and asking her not to worry.

"Alex laughed off the idea that anyone may be interested in my position," she said. "And, very solicitously, he persuaded me that keeping Anna Wintour around was in my best interests." He convinced her that if Vogue didn't keep Anna, the competition, such as Harper's Bazaar, would.

Mirabella began to suspect that her enemy was being groomed to be sent back to where she came from to head that other Vogue, and that would be the end of that. Anna later recognized that by consenting to Liberman's terms, she had "dug my grave with my blessing."

Yet, that was still several chess moves away.

Mirabella had to sit back and watch Liberman's passion for his protégée for the time being.

"He adored her beauty, hero glamor," the enraged editor-in-chief later remarked. "He was captivated by her clicking around in her high heels, trusted by and trusting no one but him." He felt her work was brilliantly modern,' combining the glamor of the 1980s with elements of street art and design. He'd frequently show up to my office and, with all the satisfaction of a cat presenting a dead mouse to its master, show me samples of art that Anna Wintour had brought in. 'Isn't this wonderful?' he'd exclaim. 'Look at what Anna did.'"

Notwithstanding Mirabella's reservations, Anna had made a visible contribution to the magazine's appearance. Anna did a sleek report on England's emerging designers that was styled by a find of hers, a young designer named Vera Wang, before being pushed out of the fashion coverage. Working with the features editor, Anna identified opportunities to improve the illustration of front-of-the-book tales in order to make them "hipper, younger," according to Schechter, who organized several of those articles. One such essay was about the East Village's gentrification and rising art and music scene. Nevertheless, as Schechter points out, "it wasn't like Anna was suggesting, 'I believe we should produce a feature on this or that.'" Instead, Anna was looking for ways to increase the visual quality of those stories. She was continuously reading domestic and foreign fashion periodicals in search of new ideas.

When it was announced that Anna would be heading to jolly old England to run Vogue and modernize "its dowdy, exclusive, and outdated-looking pages," as Mirabella put it, she patted herself on the back, thinking she'd been right all along about Anna's future, that it would be in London, not New York, and she'd finally be out of her well-coiffed hair.

Because Anna was pregnant, it was determined that she would give birth in New York and then cross the Atlantic to take on her latest adventure. Anna was due in January 1986 and was supposed to start her new job in London in April.

Her sole issue in the third trimester was early contractions, which began around Thanksgiving. She was admitted to the hospital for a few days, monitored, and given medication. "I remember David joking and saying that the main reason she went into early contractions was because the baby wanted to come out and eat," Schechter adds.

Friends in the company, people in her circle, and hangers-on began arranging rounds of lunches and dinners for her in December, not for the birth of the baby, but for her upcoming ascension to the throne of British Vogue. Her pals Michael and Tina Chow feted and fawned over her at Mr. Chow's on Fifty-seventh Street. That was a series of blows. "That was a performance of astounding discipline," one spectator said.

Anna, at the age of 37, became a mother for the first time in January, giving birth to a healthy boy called Charles in honor of her father.

There was speculation that Anna had forced Charlie's birth in order for her to attend the couture shows, which she strongly rejected through her publicist when The Times of London repeated it sixteen years later. Anna claimed she took two months off. Liz Tilberis, a fashion editor who was one of Anna's adversaries when she debuted at British Vogue, popularized the narrative.

Whatever her claim, Anna was back in her office making final arrangements for her relocation to London within what seemed like days. She asked her faithful lieutenants to join her: Schechter as her assistant once more, and Paul Sinclaire as a fashion editor. She received neither.

Sinclaire, who had irritated Anna by failing to attend her wedding because he was out of town, agreed to take the position, but then backed out, earning Anna's wrath. "She had asked me to come to English Vogue—she hadn't offered me a big job—but I had taken it, and she was counting on me." I had previously moved a lot, and I just thought it would be too much of a hassle to go to London. When I called her, she was furious. David even called to tell me, 'You best come.' Anna was furious. She was still upset with me for not attending the wedding, but my absence from English Vogue sent her over the edge. Anna perceived it as two betrayals."

Schechter, too, had reservations about traveling to London. While Anna's offer was a "wonderful opportunity," she wanted to investigate other options. Anna assigned her one month to complete the task. "I'm sure she hoped I wouldn't find any options here and would accompany her, but I just wanted to get a feel for the place."

The promised kingdom turned out to be Rolling Stone, where Schechter, then 27, became the magazine's first full-time fashion editor. Anna was quite disappointed. Later, she stated that while she "intellectually understood" Schechter's choice, "emotionally it was really difficult to take."

Anna needed to find a London assistant she could trust, someone as loyal, intelligent, and hardworking as the one she'd had since New York magazine. Anna requested suggestions. Schechter remembers having some success with an ambitious young woman named Gabe Doppelt who worked for Condé Nast in London and had done some research for her. She suggested her name, which she would later regret. Anna and Schechter would collaborate again, but this time her star would fade and Doppelt's growth.

Anna, Charles, and a full-time nanny were ensconced in a charming Victorian town house rented for her by Condé Nast in scenic and majestic Edwardes Square—with its lovely private garden in the center—in trendy Kensington by mid-March 1986. Her temporary residence, as befitting a Vogue editor, was within walking distance of the old Wintour family house in Phillimore Gardens, where Anna's love in fashion had originally blossomed two decades before.

Anna said that the practicalities of the transfer and the transatlantic marriage were "awful," and that she woke up in the middle of the night "in a cold sweat." . . 'I'm crazy,' I thought to myself. I should stay at home, care for my baby, and live a peaceful life.' But I didn't think I wanted to have a child in New York. I've been working so hard for the past fifteen years [in New York]. . . . I'd always aspired to be the editor of British Vogue. Will it be successful? In the meantime, her spouse remained in New York, and they both commuted via Concorde to visit each other. Anna's own frustration was partly directed towards her new coworkers.

The unhappiness of British Vogue's Wintour was about to begin.

Beginning of the End

Liz Tilberis and Grace Coddington were convinced that Anna was hunting them out.

Anna continually sought reshoots, adding to the pressure. Cod-first dington's had to be done three times before Anna agreed. When Coddington arrived on location, Anna instructed her to take a Polaroid of the set (before the actual shooting began) and have a courier rush it back to the office. Anna would then examine it and call Coddington, exclaiming, "Like it" or "Don't like it." If she didn't, which was often the case, Coddington would have to start over, squandering time and money.

"Anna's behavior was pure harassment and bullying," one editor claims.

Coddington was accustomed to being late—to work in the morning, and back from lunch in the afternoon—which irritated Anna, who once tracked her down to a restaurant and demanded that the former model who had controlled what appeared on Vogue's fashion pages for two decades return to the office immediately, as if she were a lowly intern.

Tilberis was tormented as well. On the morning of her father-in-burial, law's she received a slap on the wrist from Anna, who lectured her over going over budget and instructed her not to take her assistant on a planned trip to New York. Tilberis was "horrified" and felt "reprimanded like a stubborn child."

Anna was dissatisfied with anything Coddington and Tilberis thought or accomplished in the fashion world. The autocratic and tyrannical editor in chief sat in a hard-back chair during the "horribly tense" editorial meetings to decide what would go into the magazine, and if she didn't like an idea, she'd loudly tap her pencil on the desk, sending a chill through everyone present.

"She's the first female bully I've ever met," one disgruntled employee adds. Apart from her own little circle, she regarded everyone like trash. You could tell she was enjoying herself. And for what? A true tiny bully of a woman. Power was what it was all about for her. Anna's aphrodisiac is Strength. For God's sake, Vogue is just a fashion magazine, a catalog to sell clothing. And people had to be tormented so she could get a pat on the back from Liberman and Newhouse and get the role of Grace Mirabella."

Anna and the veteran editors were on opposite sides and on a dangerous collision path. "She was terrified by the type of work I was doing, the iconoclastic photos that distinguished British fashion coverage from anything in US magazines," Tilberis said. "I began to question how long I'd last and whether the anguish was worth it."

Anna trusted only a few people, including André Leon Talley, whose presence surprised her subordinates due to his flamboyant demeanor and attire: patent leather pumps, striped stretch pants, red snakeskin backpacks, and faux-fur muffs, all superimposed on this gentle black giant who, in another world, could have played for the New York Knicks with his six-foot-seven frame. But here he was at British Vogue, advising her and a few others against everything else.

Anna said that she despised almost all of the old guard's layouts, conceptions, and story ideas. Staff wanted highbrow features, but Anna wanted something in the middle. "There will always be a place for those lovely, creative mood photographs for which British Vogue is famed," Anna told a Sunday Telegraph fashion reporter, "but I would also want to see a balanced, modern approach to fashion—less drifting through the woods and more realism."

Tilberis had David Bailey snap a shot of future supermodel Christy Turlington wearing an almost open men's shirt, which Anna despised. She laced it.

Tilberis described her as "peremptory," "very tactless," "unconcerned with 'the small folks,'" "soon bored," and "didn't let anything so basic as civility get in her way." Anna's appointment, she saw as the beginning of a "rule of mediocrity."

At the collections in New York, Anna, Tilberis, and Coddington had a huge confrontation. As a gunfight began over a Ralph Lauren double-layered coat, the three were unhappy in a suite at the Algonquin Hotel, trying to pick which garments to photograph.

Coddington adored it and insisted on having it filmed. "It's fantastic," she exclaimed. Anna despised it. "It's ridiculous," she said. Tilberis explained, "It's the look." The duel raged on, with Coddington vying for "the look" and Anna constantly anticipating the reader's (and Liberman's) reaction. Tilberis panicked and began gasping for air, so she excused herself and raced out of the room. Later, she said that the stress and anxiety of the situation had prompted an asthma attack, which she would suffer from for years.

"She was a whirlwind," says former Vogue fashion editor Sophie Hicks, who left the magazine approximately six months after Anna's reign of terror began. "When Anna took over, people were surprised because she was really active and fast, and she took the position very quickly, which was quite rare." She was a breath of fresh air, working far longer hours than any previous professional with a capital 'P.' Things had been professional before Anna, but considerably more casual. She jumped right in and wanted to remake the magazine in her own image, working extraordinarily hard and expecting others to work equally hard—and they didn't mind."

Under Anna's supervision, Hicks noticed an instant improvement in the magazine's appearance and feel. The concerns had become "more coherent." . . There were isolated items of more interest. It grew less eccentric and individualistic. Some of the fashion before Anna was better than when she arrived. But, when everything is said and done, the worst of Vogue was better, but the greatest was not better."

Anna was troubled by several British attitudes, one of which was that English women, in her opinion, "are embarrassed to spend money on themselves, which is a pity," and she planned to change all of that through Vogue. "If you earn the money," she emphasized, "it is yours, and if you have a certain self-respect, it is fantastic to go out and spend it on yourself." Geraldine Ranson, who wrote the piece for the Sunday Telegraph, noted that Anna earned a large salary, so "it may take her a while to come to terms with the reality of most of her readers' domestic finances."

Coddington got the sensation that the roof had collapsed on her. She had been in charge of the magazine for several years and was now being treated cruelly. To make matters worse, she had been one of those who had first backed Anna for the post.

"Anna turned out to be cruel to her," Winston Stona, a Jamaican businessman and friend of Coddington's and Jon Bradshaw's, says. "Anna was so cruel that when I went to London and saw Grace, I told her, 'Listen, leave the bloody place.' She was horrified by how Anna treated her."

Coddington took his advice. Coddington resigned eight months after Anna assumed power. She'd had enough. "You don't need a fashion director because you're it," she declared as she handed in her resignation to become Calvin Klein's design director in New York.

Tilberis loathed Anna, yet she lobbied for Coddington's appointment. Anna paused the task and told Tilberis that if she wanted to keep her current position, let alone advance, she needed to shape up, do what she wanted her to do, stop complaining, and back her decisions and demands.

Tilberis, a power hungry woman in her own right, played ball and obtained her job a month after Coddington left.

"I never converted to Anna's themes," Tilberis later said, "but I determined right then to be a diligent number two." . . . "I did Anna's bidding directly."

Things improved significantly between them, but squabbles at the magazine persisted.

Anna was the attacker at Vogue, yet she was cast as the victim by the British press. She had grown to despise the media. She considered herself a journalist, the daughter of a well-known one, and she had been romantically associated with many in the past—yet in private and then in public, she blasted Fleet Street. "The British press are the worst," she claimed in 2002, while addressing her treatment at British Vogue.

Everything about her became a point of contention. The Evening Standard, her father's old newspaper, sent a reporter to interview her, and the story claimed that Anna had offered the scribe a "Valium. . . to soothe my anxiety," that Anna's grin "looks fleeting and fake," that Anna was "not quite British" after a decade in New York, and that her primary interest was in articles about "professional women, business suits, and working out." . . . 'A new type of woman is emerging. She is fascinated by business and money. She no longer has time to go shopping. 'She wants to know what, why, where, and how,' Anna stated. 'Therefore I believe that the fashion pages, in addition to looking great, should include information.'"

"Is there anything pleasant to say about Anna?" queried the Evening Standard. Friends describe her as a pushover—a mug for men who can take a joke. . ."

The British press were not the only ones who were critical of her.

Anna, according to the New York Times, "is a thorn in the side of London's stylish set, who think the magazine has become too bland." Anna's response? "Any reply is better than no reaction," she said, adding, "A new editor will revolutionize a magazine." Humans are resistant to change. British fashion was somewhat exclusive. It has to be opened."

Someone created a button criticizing Anna's radical redesign of the magazine about the same time the press was going after her. Thom O'Dwyer, the style editor of London's Fashion Weekly, was seen wearing one in a trendy London restaurant. It said, "Vogue. Vague. Vomit."

But Anna has bigger issues. Tilberis, her second in command, had become the target of a fierce headhunt by Ralph Lauren and Calvin Klein, who both wanted her to travel to New York and assume important tasks with them in the aftermath of Coddington's desertion. Lauren had been the first to call, but when Tilberis sworn Coddington to secrecy and informed her of Lauren's $250,000 offer, Coddington went straight to her employer, and the next thing Tilberis knew, Klein was courting her as well.

When Tilberis went to Anna's office in June 1987 to submit her resignation, Anna was horrified and proceeded to disparage Seventh Avenue and its aristocrats, such as Lauren and Klein. Tilberis, on the other hand, had already accepted Lauren's offer, the press had reported that she was accompanying Coddington to America, and friends were arranging farewell parties. Her family was packed and ready to travel, she said Anna, their house had been sold.

Anna dialed Newhouse and Liberman's numbers.

Tilberis (and soon the fashion world) received the shock of their lives a few days later. In a private meeting, Anna revealed in confidence that she was the one leaving British Vogue, and she offered Tilberis her job, which she accepted right away.

Speculation concerning Anna's likely resignation from Vogue and her future in America had been circulating since early 1987, around the time rumors in the press revealed she was pregnant again.

One piece about the hypothesis in The New York Times caused tensions in the Condé Nast executive suite on Madison Avenue. "It is probable that Anna Wintour may come to the United States, within a specific length of time," fashion columnist Michael Gross concluded in a column, adding, "That should keep the rumors swirling."

As he returned to his desk the next morning, he found a succession of frantic phone messages from Liberman. The reporter called immediately, and Liberman's first words were, "Dear friend, it appears that we have gotten me into some trouble." What are we going to do to get me out of this situation? " According to Gross, Liberman gave the distinct sense that he had been chastised for his remark, most likely by Newhouse, and that he was now requesting a correction."

"Obviously, he'd been read the riot act that morning," Gross says, "and it took me 45 minutes to talk him out of the correction, which I did by explaining to him that by the end of the day, his parakeet will be shitting on the story, and if there's a correction, all you're going to do is keep this alive." It's far better to let it go."

Anna's second child was due on July 30, and she planned to work until the 29th. "It's not a sickness," she insisted to the Daily Mail. Anna got a scan and discovered it was a girl.

The speculation about Anna leaving Vogue began shortly after Si Newhouse, who was aware of her mounting dissatisfaction, flew to London for a brunch meeting with her. He intended to cheer her up, convince her that her time will come, and offer her a new position in

New York.

Anna thought this was the big moment she'd been waiting for, when Newhouse handed her the editorship of American Vogue.

The rumor that something major was going to happen to Anna was confirmed in mid-August.

She was returning to New York, but not to Vogue to topple Grace Mirabella, but to Home & Garden, Condé Nast's respected shelter magazine. Lou Gropp, the magazine's longtime editor in chief, was fired three days after Anna's appointment was announced. "Lou was sacked extremely harshly," claims a former high-ranking editor at Home & Garden. "He was on vacation in California and called the office every day until one day he called from a public phone in a parking lot and Si told him he was history."

Anna was "completely startled," as she subsequently stated, by Newhouse's offer, and not joyfully stunned, because she could nearly taste American Vogue.

"I walked directly back to the office and contacted Alex, and he said, " Yeah, you have to come."

She put on a happy front for The New York Times, saying little of substance and speaking only on the condition that she not be asked about her plans for her new magazine—mainly because she didn't have any. "I've really missed New York," she admitted. "I'm really looking forward to coming back," she said of her time in London, adding, "Some people didn't like what I did."

By the time Anna took over, British Vogue had been through the most traumatic period in its seven decades: more than two-thirds of the staff had been replaced, she had banned lunchtime drinking, and she made sure her top editors arrived at eight a.m. by sending cars to pick them up, most of whom arrived rather bleary. It wasn't quite the

Blitz, but it seemed like it to those who worked in the trenches at Vogue. While the style and feel had changed during Anna's brief, contentious reign, circulation and advertising remained about the same.

"Everyone was happy when she gained the editorship of Home & Garden," says Drusilla Beyfus Shulman, "because every editor at British Vogue could breathe safely."

Anna justified, defended, and denied some of the changes she implemented during her time in London. She stated that everyone at Vogue "thought I was some sort of American control freak," that the press presented her as a "witch of steel," and that "I only remember letting two or three people go." But, very doubt fearing my terrible reputation, a lot of people fled on their own."

She claimed she was attacked because she decided to "infuse the magazine with a bit of American worldliness, even toughness," and that the magazine's "cozy but mildly eccentric atmosphere" struck her as "out of date" and "out of step," as well as "not responsive to intelligent women's changing lives."

Anna had a baby girl in early August 1987, as planned, whom the Shaffers called Kate but nicknamed Bee, primarily because when she first started talking, the toddler had difficulty expressing her actual name, mumbling something like "bah-bee," so Bee it became. Anna was back in the workplace three days after giving birth, according to Fleet Street. Yet, according to Anna's brother James, there was such concern about the baby's health that Nonie flew over from England to be by her side. But the emergency dissipated quickly.

Six weeks later, on September 9, Anna began redesigning her new magazine. Already, rumor was rife that she would stay at Home & Garden for a brief reprieve before yanking the rug out from under Grace Mirabella.

Liz Tilberis, the new editor in chief of British Vogue, resurrected that shot Anna had murdered of Christy Turlington and put it on her debut cover the first day Anna was out of her hair. She and her family celebrated Anna's long-awaited departure with a traditional English meal of takeout fish and chips washed down with pricey champagne.

The Party's Over

Anna transformed Vogue into her image of what a great fashion magazine should be, from evicting seasoned staffers to igniting in-house competition for articles to instituting dress requirements and strange norms of behavior.

Other long-term employees fled in fear or disgust at the changes or their treatment, as Grace Coddington had done in London before returning to the fold. Others left because their departments were disbanded, they were laid off, or they retired.

"Anna had a very intriguing method of establishing herself," says Elizabeth Tretter, a seventeen-year Vogue veteran. Anna demolished the fabric department's hierarchy in order to streamline the business. "She looked at the current employees and arranged meals with those she wanted to keep, and if you didn't have lunch with her, you knew what was up."

Tretter was lucky enough to receive an invitation, and Anna brought her to Tretter's favorite restaurant, the Oyster Bar at Grand Central Station. They enjoyed a great conversation, but Tretter was soon gone.

"Age could have been a role," she argues, noting that she was a decade older than Anna and that "Anna's mandate was young, lively, and enthusiastic." Gabriel Doppelt, a hip-hop editor, was brought in. I wasn't into hip-hop."

Tretter's department had been closed, and she had been handed the laborious task of shooting pattern papers, which everyone despised.

Tretter had discussed all of Anna's comments about wanting everything youthful to a younger acquaintance, who thought "that is actionable" and indicated that an age-discrimination suit, similar to what had transpired at HG, would be in order. "But that was the extent of it," she recalls. "Did I get pushed out? Perhaps, given the current state of affairs."

Tretter had built numerous contacts in the fabric industry during her time at Vogue, so when things began to seem bad, she had options outside of Vogue. "I told my husband, 'I guess the party is over.' I went to see Anna and told her I needed to go somewhere else." She never said, 'No, you can't leave.'"

Another older, long-time editor, who departed six months into Anna's tenure but remained with Condé Nast, believed age had a role in Anna's personnel decisions as well. "There was the entire young, young, young thing," she claims. "Anna was sort of peeling everyone who was older out." Anna was simply insistent that everyone be youthful. And the point is, she inherited Polly Mellen, who is far from youthful. Polly, on the other hand, overcame the age barrier since she was such a character and worked so hard."

Mellen, who had worked at Vogue for over three decades, had been Anna's closest supporter during Grace Mirabella's reign and was the one who set up that fateful meeting in which Anna told Mirabella she wanted her job. Anna was aware of Mellen's support, and Mellen was the first person she informed of Grace Codding-arrival. ton's "I got a call from Anna saying, 'I want you to be the first to know,' and she informed me Grace was going to be creative director, and she asked, 'Do you like her?'" Do you guys get along? 'I adore her,' I told her."

Mellen and Coddington were expected to collaborate closely. But, over time, fewer and fewer of Mellen's sittings and ideas were published in the magazine, until none were.

"It was sad in a way," a colleague recalls. "Polly sat there with her thumb up her you-know-what." Nothing from her work made it into the book. Anna and Grace were conveying a message to her."

Mellen says she was aware of Anna's objective to have everyone "young and beautiful," but she believed that "performance was still number one," and she came to the harsh truth that "two powerful editors," like her and Coddington, working together "doesn't work."

Mellen hung in there as long as she could, hoping for the best, but the writing was on the wall: "I began to feel like I'm not really doing shots, maybe I'm not really young enough for Anna." When the time comes, you can feel it, and I'm really good at it. 'Come on, you've had a lovely life,' I had to remark after some serious soul-searching. You're the fashion world's spoiled brat."

Anna had concluded that she had given Mellen enough rope and that it was now time to carefully lower the trapdoor.

Si Newhouse took care of the task for her. He summoned Mellen to his office and inquired about her ideal work. "At my advanced age, I replied, if you can believe it, I'd like my own magazine."

He didn't have that to share, but he did tell Mellen that Linda Wells at Allure was looking for a creative director to replace Laurie Schechter.

Unlike many of her contemporaries, Mellen made the journey and built a space for herself there. And she credits Anna for having "guts, passion, bravery, caring, a point of view, and, most importantly, absolute focus." She has had the greatest influence on fashion in the twentieth century. She ranks beside Coco Chanel in my opinion. People may disagree with me, but I'm a fan."

Everything changed when Anna took over.

There were numerous lengthy sessions while Mirabella headed the show. "I remember sitting in a Grace run-through and it was like,

'Oh, my God, tell us what you want for heaven's sake," recalls one editor who was close to Mirabella and despised Anna. It's not brain surgery.' Then you went, Huh, with Anna. . . The meetings were over in a second, so this is far too easy. It went from one extreme to the other. Anna was never late; she was always on time. You used to stick around for a long time."

Michael Roberts, a longtime British friend of Anna's who became The New Yorker's fashion editor under Tina Brown in the mid-1990s, had observed Anna closely over the years and concluded that she "just prefers to keep things terse, short, and to the point."

Anna's dictatorial demeanor was evident even in Vogue's elevators and halls.

Toby Young, a British journalist who worked as a contributing editor at Vanity Fair in the mid-1990s, claimed there was an "unwritten rule" that Anna didn't allow anyone to travel in the elevators with her and that staffers "were expected to let her go first and take the next one."

He remembered a jokester who worked as a researcher at Vanity Fair talking about hiding behind a pillar in the lobby, waiting for Anna to emerge, and then "piling in with her" when she got on the elevator. His act would be carried out after consuming a lot of beans and beer the night before.

There was even a regulation about how Anna should be addressed and when and where she may be approached.

The teenage daughter of a Vogue department head had gotten a summer internship and had been cautioned by her mother not to speak to "Ms. Wintour." The girl was walking down the corridor one day when she noticed Anna coming her way. She went rapidly and looked straight ahead, fearful of a confrontation with the boss woman, according to Young's story, hoping they would pass safely like two ships in the night. But just as they were about to meet, one of Anna's high heels gave way and she fell to the floor, falling at the girl's feet. She "gently stepped over Anna's prostrate figure," remembering what her mother had instructed her, and hurried to her mother's office, where the kid was informed she'd done "the right thing."

"Here, at last, was Patsy from Absolutely Fabulous in the flesh," Young said as he beheld Anna.

Everything was a team effort under Mirabella, and decisions were decided by committee, which took a long time. The idea was assigned to the person who came up with it. Everything changed dramatically under Anna.

"Everyone was sort of an Indian, off doing their own stories, with a smaller story pot to chose from," recalls one editor who left in less than a year because she couldn't deal with Anna's demands and warp-speed drive.

"There would be a list of designers, and each editor would, of course, want the same thing," she recalls. "So you'd be screaming, 'Me, me, me!' Please, please, please.' It was both amusing and heartbreaking. We were like kids. They were squabbling. You'd bring in an accessory to use and hide it away from everyone else in a closet. . . . Because everyone was competing for a piece of the turf, you had to start wearing body armor. Anna basically let the powerful people in there do their thing. It felt like the dinosaur period was coming to an end."

Anna hired fresh authors. Some survived, but others did not. One of the latter was Ed Kosner's wife, magazine writer and novelist Julie Baumgold, who had unsuccessfully tried to keep Anna in New York when she was being courted by Alex Liberman.

Anna thought Baumgold could handle the celebrity stories she was suddenly cramming into the magazine, some worthy, others perplexing, like the makeover layouts featuring tabloid figures like Lisa Marie Presley and Ivana Trump.

Baumgold's first job in the late 1990s was a profile of Brad Pitt. "I'd never met Brad Pitt, but I wrote a fast essay about him since they had some great Brad Pitt photos—and nobody altered a word," Baumgold adds. "That was sort of male beauty, and I noted that Marilyn Monroe and Elvis had nose jobs, and Brad Pitt had a small scar on his cheek."

That was Anna's type of art. She was overjoyed, and she asked Baumgold to lunch.

"She invited me to be a contributing editor, and I said yes because of that experience [writing about Brad Pitt]."

Baumgold's last pleasant experience was working for Anna at Vogue.

She claims that her subsequent interactions with the editor in chief were "never forthright." It was constantly coming through other people, which was a mistake. 'This is what Anna wants,' it was often said. . And that wasn't the ideal method to filter things. That wasn't direct, and I never really understood it because it changed all the time."

Baumgold was urged to include Kate Beckinsale in an article on femme fatales because "Anna wants you to include Kate Beckinsale, Anna wants this, Anna wants that." . ."

After a few more pieces, it all became too much for Baumgold to handle. "I worked for Anna for six months before I couldn't take it anymore and quit," she laughs at the memories. "That was the last time I had fun working in journalism." I left. That was the end of my story. This was a stumbling block in my magazine career."

While Baumgold made the cut with Anna but couldn't deal with her indirect demands, others felt that the magazine's corporate culture and journalistic direction weren't a good fit and left.

That was the case with highly regarded fashion reporter Robin Givhan, who contributed to The Washington Post's vivacious Style column.

Anna, who knew Givhan and had interviewed her for fashion features over the years, approached her about becoming an assistant editor, a position that had recently become available. Givhan was humbled and thought to himself, "If I'm ever going to write full-time about fashion for a magazine, it's not going to get any better than Vogue."

Givhan has always admired Anna, particularly her "amazing decisiveness," noting, "I would interview her, and there's never any hesitancy, always a really firm opinion, thought out, always supported." I'd approach her about having Hillary [Clinton] or Oprah on the cover. . . . She had a clear picture of why those covers were important. . . see how such decisions would have a cascading effect within popular culture. She can discuss it in a way that goes beyond simply discussing clothes."

Givhan accepted to join the squad when Anna pursued him. Givhan observes, "Anna is quite good at getting what she wants." "She has a lot of charisma."

Yet after a few months, Givhan began to have reservations about the position, asking whether Anna was the employer she wanted to work for and whether Vogue was the right location for her.

One of the reasons was the magazine's lack of objectivity. Givhan rapidly learned that the emphasis of every item she wrote or considered had to "be modified to meet the Vogue point of view."

Givhan was well aware that a publication like The Post chose persons to be interviewed based on diversity, whereas the rule of thumb at Vogue was far narrower.

"You want women with a sophisticated point of view—not a suburban soccer mom, but rather a suburban charity worker." You're always wondering what these women look like. They'll be photographed, so they should reflect a Vogue sensibility."

Writing for Vogue, Givhan thought, "was preaching to the choir, those interested in fashion, not women with an estranged connection with fashion."

One story that piqued Givhan's interest and which she suggested to Anna never saw the light of day. It was about a designer who had a bad image in the fashion world, was hated and self-destructive, but nonetheless excelled and received popular acclaim. "I felt it would make an intriguing story and provide insight into what goes on behind the scenes."

But Anna wasn't convinced.

"The aim of Vogue is to praise the business, not to tear it down," Givhan says. "My story was not a happy one. Fashion creativity is taken seriously by Vogue. It values its readers' interest in fashion. A woman who simply loves shoes is readily criticized, but the magazine does not do so. 'You know what?' they say. You like shoes, we like shoes, and there's nothing wrong with it."

Givhan had had enough of it after four months. When she revealed to a friend that she was considering quitting, she was urged, "Honey, buck up. There are people out there who would slaughter an entire crowd for your job."

Givhan resigned after six months, leaving on good terms with Anna, and returning to her fashion beat at The Washington Post.

Anna has formed good relationships with The Washington Post. Katharine Graham, the owner, and Anna's father were friends. And Anna had become friends with Nina Hyde, a long-time fashion editor who died of breast cancer, a cause Anna was very passionate about. As a result, when it came to selecting editors and writers, she tended to favor Post employees. Stephanie Mansfield, who gained a reputation in the Post's Style section for her acerbic tales and profiles of politicians and celebrities, was hired as a contract writer by Anna. Their relationship also didn't last long.

One of her responsibilities was to write a profile of designer Donna Karan that was harsh on her by Vogue standards—not critical, but honest, dealing with her personal connections, among other things.

"Maybe Anna didn't read the story before it got in," says Nancy McKeon, who worked with Anna at New York magazine and was Mansfield's Washington Post colleague. "Anna took Stephanie out to lunch and was trying to tell her, you know, we have to be careful with these folks." "I don't know what those girls think they're doing up there, but it sure isn't journalism," Stephanie said to me.

Then there were individuals who were so desperate to work at Vogue yet so afraid of Anna that they found themselves lying to her in order to be hired.

Candace Bushnell, a blond, leggy, men-on-the-brain writer, labeled the editor in chief as "one of the scariest women in the world," in one example of fabrication-for-Anna's-sake. "I don't give a damn what anyone says."

Anna had offered Bushnell a position, and the two had gone out to lunch to finalize the transaction when the white lie surfaced.

"She's eating a gory steak, like it was just slain in the street and brought in." I'm attempting to consume a lamb chop. "I'm shaking,"

Bushnell recalled. "'Oh, Candace, you are perfectly our demographic,' she says. You live in a city and are thirty-two.' I was like, 'OK, I'm thirty-two.'

"I was actually thirty-six years old. But I was so afraid of her that I didn't want to reveal my age because I was afraid I'd be fired before I even started writing this column. So I began dating the publisher. So I couldn't tell him [her true age] because I'd already lied to Anna, and they talked all the time, so it would've come out."

Bushnell, who penned what became HBO's blockbuster Sex and the City as a columnist for the New York Observer, described her Anna experience as "one of these horrifying situations you never ever imagine you'll get in" (A friend of hers tipped gossip columns and her real age eventually surfaced.)

Anna also killed stories that were not attractive, slim, and beautiful. "Have you seen her? She's monstrous-looking." "One well-known star," an editor recalls Anna stating.

Similarly, Anna is reported to have destroyed an article by a tremendously accomplished author after seeing his photo in the piece and deciding he wasn't attractive enough to adorn her pages. The piece's editor is alleged to have argued with Anna, but to no avail, that it was all about the writer's words, not his looks.

Anna may appear arrogant to big fashion stars such as red-carpet diva Cindy Crawford.

Crawford, who was supposed to be on the September cover, was forced to attend three separate shooting sessions since Anna wasn't happy with her look. Anna, in the end, murdered the Crawford cover. When the model's representatives objected, they were told, "Cindy Crawford is just another model." Hello, my name is Anna Wintour. "

Under Anna, the cover featured more celebrities and fewer well-known models. In 1998, for example, Anna put Liz Hurley, Sandra Bullock, Claire Danes, the Spice Girls, Renée Zellweger (whose fashion look Anna would control until 2004), Oprah Winfrey (Anna demanded she lose significant weight before appearing on the cover, and the queen of daytime TV obliged), and Hillary Clinton on the cover of Vogue. "Supermodel Carolyn Murphy, the August cover girl, truly felt out of place in their company," said The Guardian in London.

Anna would continue the trend, and by the turn of the millennium, celebrities featured the majority of Vogue covers.

Anna had hired Laurie Jones, one of her biggest supporters at New York magazine and a two-decade veteran of the weekly, as her new managing editor.

Jones was so taken with Anna's portfolio that she brought her to the attention of Ed Kosner, the editor, who hired her on the spot and gave her the exposure that drew Alexander Liberman's attention at Vogue. And it was Jones who told Anna, in an attempt to persuade her to stay, "You can't leave New York; you're the only one doing fashion." You'll be lost if you go to Vogue.' I knew it would be difficult to replace her.``

Jones was now working for Anna and was still her loyal lieutenant a dozen years later, in 2004.

Jones began her career at Vogue the day after the 1992 presidential election, and she recalls how excited Anna was to see William and Hillary Clinton succeed George Bush. "Anna had been out at several parties," Jones remembers, "and she was really thrilled that he'd won."

Anna was fascinated by Clinton's charisma and sexiness, and she recognized the bad boy in him that she had always found appealing in men. Bill and Hillary were celebrities as well as savvy politicians, Anna felt, because they weathered the Gennifer Flowers incident and were elected. "Anna told me the Clintons were the new Kennedys and the royal family rolled into one," a Vogue editor wrote at the time.

The first lady was concerned about her appearance as the Monica Lewinsky sex scandal emerged. She was never into fashion. She wore navy blue pantsuits and low shoes to cover her overweight legs as a Beltway wonk, her hair was a catastrophe, and she had those terrifying brows. The president's wife realized she needed a major makeover. She began meeting with celebrity hairstylist Cristophe and conferred with haute-couture king Oscar de la Renta, who entrusted her to Anna's capable hands. They became good buddies.

Hillary's outfit became more stylish, even glamorous, under Anna's tutelage—and Anna had an objective going in. She started wearing neutral-colored suits with long jackets to hide her large hips, her hair turned blonder and straighter, and she started wearing softer matte makeup. Anna scoffed at the appearances of some of the other female characters in the Clinton saga, including Monica Lewinsky and Linda Tripp. "You'd better have a nice hairdresser if you're going to make accusations against the president," she insisted.

Anna's deft interaction with the first lady and future New York senator culminated in a significant scoop for Vogue.

During the politically tense Ken Starr vs. Bill Clinton year of 1998, Anna placed a glamorous new Hillary Clinton on the cover of the December edition, marking the first time a first lady had ever struck a pose there. There she was, the president's stand-by-your-man wife, confident and self-assured in a velvet gown and perfectly coiffed.

Hillary Clinton's sitting sparked so much worldwide coverage that Vogue's PR department sent out a binder volume of tear sheets. On newsstands alone, the issue sold over a million copies.

"The press was all over it before the issue was even published," Anna told The New York Times. "Many saw it as vindication for [Hillary Clinton] because being on the cover of Vogue transcends power and politics." That demonstrates that she is a powerful lady and an idol of American women."

Anna was ecstatic about her acquaintance with one of the country's most fascinating first ladies since Jackie. So proud, in fact, that she returned to New York with a stack of souvenir White House stationery following one of her visits to the Clinton White House. During a future visit to London, she presented some of the letterheads and envelopes to her brother Patrick, a political reporter at The Guardian, who found her admiration for the first family hilarious. "Patrick makes fun of Anna," claims Patti Gilkyson Agnew, Anna's cousin. "He wrote me a letter on White House stationery with the words, 'This is from Anna, and Anna's love of Hillary Clinton.' He claimed Anna brought the stationery over and left it,'so don't assume I'm writing you from the White House.'"

Linda Wells of Allure entered the Clinton race with an issue showcasing a makeover of another of the commander in chief's women, the Minnie Mouse-like, big-haired Paula Jones. Not to be outdone, Tina Brown put "that woman, Ms. Lewinsky" on the cover of Vanity Fair, and a year later, Brown had Hillary Clinton addressing her husband's infidelity in the first issue of her new magazine, Talk.

But it was Anna who first recognized the Clintons' star power and won the Condé Nast competition.

Laurie Jones portrays Anna as a sort of superwoman. "She's really stoic and powerful," she says. "She has no fear. Everything is completed in a timely manner. There are numerous encounters, but none of them last long. Anna does everything with ease. She gives her approval to all the tale ideas. She goes through the motions of bringing in all the clothes on the rack. She chooses the images as they arrive."

Anna's schedule was demanding. She normally got up at six a.m. and played a good game of tennis before getting her hair and makeup done professionally. Around eight a.m., she had rounds of meetings and made dozens of quick editorial decisions before going out for a high-protein lunch of a lamb chop or a hamburger, hoping she didn't run into the animal rights activists who have constantly gone after her, once even throwing a dead raccoon in her plate, which Anna nonchalantly pushed aside and continued with her chopped steak, seemingly unfazed. She normally left the workplace about six o'clock, and her evenings were just as busy as her days. There were charity events she had to attend—Anna has generously donated her time as a fashion powerhouse to AIDS awareness and breast cancer research. She had to make an appearance at a few parties.

When she saw the cameras directed at her, she transformed from ice queen to glamour queen, preening, posing, and smiling. There are literally thousands of images of her posing for the cameras and modeling every expensive dress imaginable, many of which were given to her by friendly designers.

Every night throughout an issue closing cycle, she had to go over and approve stories and images in the "book"—a precious, heavy, bound volume that an assistant delivered to her house. The layouts are shown in the order in which they appeared in the magazine. The following morning, Anna's bible is returned to the art department.

"Anna has gone through every layout, every page, and the pages are covered with her Post-it notes after she's reviewed everything," Jones says. "There might be a collage of several images and something the size of a postage stamp, and Anna could say she doesn't like that dress, that whoever is wearing it wore it to such and such a party on such and such a date." Her attention to detail is astounding to me."

Anna, according to Jones, "takes home manuscripts every night and reads everything that comes into the magazine."

Almost everything, to be precise.

Patricia Bosworth's biography of her father, Bartley Crum, was released in 1997, after a decade of research. Bosworth's father's eventful career as a high-powered lawyer, his work as an adviser to Harry Truman, his struggle against the Hollywood blacklist, and his suicide in 1959 at the age of fifty-nine had all been written about.

Everything Your Little Heart Desires, like her biographies of Montgomery Clift and Diane Arbus, was warmly received and received a full-page review by Mary Cantwell in the book section of Vogue's April 1997 edition.

"Vogue reviewed my book beautifully, which was, of course, quite helpful," recalls Bosworth.

Although Bosworth's book was not a best-seller, the author did get a Survivor of the Year Award from the American Foundation for Suicide Prevention, a group in which David Shaffer was active due to his expertise in teen suicides.

Some months after the assessment was published, the organization's annual awards banquet was held at a New York hotel. "Judy Collins performed for me," adds Bosworth, who was sitting at a table with Anna and her husband and couldn't help but note that they had "no relationship" and "didn't converse to one another."

"Since Vogue had given me such a large spread, I naturally leaned over and thanked Anna." Yet she had no idea what I was referring to.

"She informed me she hadn't read my book and had no idea the review was in her magazine," says Bosworth. "I assumed she'd read it, but she didn't know anything about it, which astonished me given that she's the editor in chief." That struck me, and I'm not an egomaniac."

A few months later, Bosworth ran into Richard David Storey, the Vogue features editor who had overseen her book's assessment, and informed him what had happened.

"I just said to myself, 'I can't believe this.'" 'My God, she didn't read it.' That's when I realized it wasn't an isolated incident. 'Oh, yeah, it's par for the course,' he said. She never, or only very rarely, reads the copy for books and movies—the arts stuff.' I found that utterly astounding."

Together with her editorial responsibilities, Anna delegated to Laurie Jones the task of interviewing possible assistants.

Few people were ever as hardworking, dutiful, or ambitious as Laurie Schechter or Gabe Doppelt, therefore Anna had a lot of them. Anna, on the other hand, enjoyed some of them. "She takes good care of her assistants," Jones says proudly. "Anna is loyal to them. One went on to become the sittings editor's assistant."

Yet one in particular proved to be a major source of concern for Anna.

She was a tall, pretty, preppy blonde fresh out of college who aspired to be a writer—a Vogue model, it seemed. Lauren Weisberger was her name.

"I was the one who hired Lauren Weisberger," Jones admits.

Jones made a brave statement since Weisberger's name, if uttered and overheard by Anna in the hallowed corridors of Vogue, could lead to a career decapitation.

Weisberger worked as Anna's assistant for less than a year. Once she departed, she wrote The Devil Wears Prada, a novel à clef about her time as an assistant to the barely fictional Miranda Priestly, the editor in chief of a fashion magazine named Runway, who was hailed as the most revered—and despised—woman in fashion.

Although Weisberger denied it repeatedly, everyone in the exclusive world of fashion knew that Miranda and Anna were the same person; only the names were altered to protect the guilty and the author from legal punishment.

The book, part of the chick lit genre written and read by young women, became a hit in 2003, following in the footsteps of The Nanny Diaries, a dramatized tell-all published by two former short-term nannies who worked for wealthy East Side Manhattan mothers. These were precursors of The Bergdorf Blondes, a 2004 best-seller about stunning Manhattan man-hunters written by a former Vogue journalist and Anna's British friend. The books catered to the same population of twenty- and thirty-somethings who dreamt about having glamorous lives with studly lovers while watching Melrose Place, Friends, and Sex and the City.

The Devil Wears Prada received a glowing review from Publishers Weekly: "As the 'lowest-paid-but-most-highly-perked assistant in the free world,' [Andrea Sachs, the protagonist] soon learns that her Nine West loafers won't cut it—everyone wears Jimmy Choos or Manolos—and that the four years she spent memorizing poems and examining prose won't help her in her new role of 'finding, fetching . . . Weisberger has written a comedic novel that has risen to the top of the chick-lit category."

The Daily Telegraph in London dubbed the genre "Boss Betrayal," citing Miranda Priestly as "a stick-thin, British, steak-eating, tennis-playing, fur-and-Prada-wearing editrix with two children, who resembles Wintour in every observable way except that she invariably sports a white Hermès scarf, whereas Wintour is known for her sunglasses."

According to the story, Weisberger "gives the real Anna Wintour a walk-on part" in order to avoid a lawsuit.

Many of the reviews and articles written about the caustic novel were sympathetic to Anna. Some journalists thought the book was unjust. "Wintour is tough in her position, you have to be," according to The Telegraph piece, which seemed to represent the sentiments of many others on both sides of the Atlantic. You must also be dedicated, hardworking, fashion-obsessed, and self-disciplined."

Hilary Alexander, the newspaper's fashion editor, was reported in the piece as stating, "I'm sure she [Anna] is probably rather difficult to work with, but she needs to be." She most likely makes things difficult for her assistants at times due to her strong will. It's the nature of the trade. Fashion is full of workaholics who devote their entire life to it because they adore it."

With all the attention, Anna had to say something, so she told The New York Times, "I am looking forward to reading the book." Her European editor at large, Hamish Bowles, said the book should be dismissed as "quite inventive fiction."

Anna was enraged privately. "She was spouting fire," a Vogue editor says. "Anna thought Weisberger had used and abused her."

Aside from providing Weisberger her fifteen minutes, the book cemented Anna's place in the public celebrity pantheon. Anna was now known and spoken about over Big Macs and fries under the Golden Arches by young fashionistas in Wal-Mart jeans in Davenport and Dubuque, in addition to the glittering venues of New

York, London, Paris, and Milan.

Weisberger "wasn't here very long," says Laurie Jones, who claims she never read the book. "She went with him when Richard Storey departed," the editor revealed to Patricia Bosworth that Anna didn't read anything in her magazine. She wanted to work in features, but there weren't many openings, so she asked to work as Richard's assistant. She appeared to be a totally happy, attractive woman when she was here."

Jones had to do a lot of interviewing to fill the post vacated by a more recent assistant of Anna's who was promoted. "Everyone had read the book," she explains. "One of them asked if she had to walk Anna's dog." No, I said. That's probably in the book.

"Anna doesn't divulge many facts about her personal life," Jones admits. "She's a little cryptic, and she doesn't open up to people." Some have questions about her, including the phrase "nuclear Wintour." We go our separate ways, but we can always chat about stuff."

A New Life

The cruelest month for Anna was November 1999, on the eve of the new millennium.

Even in the best of circumstances—and those were the worst—she was dreading it.

November was a significant milestone in her life: she turned five.

Approaching fifty was especially difficult for Anna, whose entire being and attitude, both for herself and for Vogue, was built on looking young—model young, movie star gorgeous young, miniskirt and Manolos sexy young.

But now she was fifty years old, entangled in a horrifying, very public extramarital affair and a horrific divorce. Furthermore, she was anxious about the longevity of her relationship because her partner had been on and off her radar in previous months.

"Shelby was cooling his heels," one insider claims. "Katherine had previously caught Shelby. He'd apologized and promised not to do it again if she accepted him back. He was caught again, this time with Anna, and he was apologizing loudly. I don't think he wanted to divorce his wife for Anna at the time."

According to another reliable source, "Shelby was not the epitome of the monogamous person, and Katherine knew it." He was known as a ladies' guy. Katherine knew Shelby had hooked up with Anna from the beginning, but I don't think Katherine ever imagined it would lead to anything."

For a time, it was thought that Anna and Bryan had broken up, and that Anna was attempting to reconcile with an enraged David Shaffer.

When a lady writer friend of Jon Bradshaw's who also knew Anna first saw Bryan, she was taken aback by his likeness to Bradshaw and how similar they acted around women. "I met Shelby at my literary agent's place one night, and he was already with Anna and flirted with me." It was impossible for me to believe! "

Anna celebrated her 50th birthday on Wednesday, November 3.

The next day, she received a phone call from her brother Patrick in London. Anna's father, the most influential person in her life, whose chilly demeanor and editing style she inherited and mimicked, had died at home in Tisbury, Wiltshire. Audrey, his second wife, was by his side. Wintour was 82 years old when he died of cerebral arteriosclerosis, or hardening of the arteries in his brain.

Coupled with all the turmoil in her life, Anna was now overcome with grief over her father's death.

"She was devastated, in astonishment," a longtime family friend said. "First, there was all of the dreadful talk about her affair, and then her father died." It was too much, even for Anna, who is as solid as the Rock of Gibralter. Charles was the most powerful man in Anna's life. He was her teacher, her mentor, and her counselor. She was severe, austere, frigid, and innovative, much like him. It's a cliche, but she was truly Daddy's girl.``

Her parents had both left her. Nonie died three years before, on January 5, 1996, eight days before her 79th birthday. The divorced, lonely, and retired social worker died while being treated at London's prestigious Royal Brompton and National Heart Hospital for pneumonia and a preleukemia blood cell disease. Friends from her previous marriage, such as film critic Alex Walker, were not even notified of her death. One of their infrequent encounters, according to an American cousin, was when Anna called to inform her of her mother's death. A tiny memorial service was held in London. Prior to her hospitalization, Nonie Wintour was living in a flat in Chelsea with Patrick Wintour and his wife, Madeleine Bunting Wintour, also a Guardian journalist, who kept an eye on her. The pair eventually divorced.

Anna left everything and traveled to London to handle funeral arrangements (he was cremated) and a memorial service after learning of her father's death.

In its obituary, The Guardian stated, "If the test of a competent editor is the capacity to imprint a new sense of style and purpose on a newspaper, then Charles Wintour." . . He was widely regarded as one of the greatest editors of the second part of the twentieth century. . . A courtly gentleman with a keen pen and an even sharper private tongue. . . . People who worked with him did not always love him, but he was universally respected for his shrewdness and quick decision-making. He was the general in every battle, with military precision."

When Anna learned a disturbing clause in her father's will, her anguish turned to rage.

The document was dated August 23, 1993, when Anna and David Shaffer, whom Charles Always always considered a "saint," were still together. "I DO NOT LEAVE A SHARE OF MY RESIDUARY ESTATE TO MY DAUGHTER ANNA WINTOUR SHAFFER AS SHE IS WELL PROVIDED FOR," the clause stated, "but I want her to know that I am very proud of her great success and achievement, and I am equally pleased that she has combined her career so happily with her family life."

Anna's joyful family life was now a distant memory.

And, much to Anna's disgust, her father's fortune, worth millions of dollars in stocks, shares, and personal and real estate, was bequeathed to his widow, whom she despised; the widow's two children from a previous marriage; and Anna's three siblings.

Anna was more concerned that she wasn't an heir than that her stepmother and her father's stepchildren were beneficiaries.

Anna returned to New York with a memorial service for her father planned for December, only to be struck with yet another painful blow.

Alex Liberman, who discovered Anna's abilities and was the dominating creative and political force in steering her career through Condé Nast to the pinnacle at Vogue, died on November 20 at his retirement home in Florida. He was 87 years old. For Anna, who owed her career to Liberman, his death came as a rude awakening just two weeks after her father's.

November appeared to be a cursed month in Anna's privileged society. Jon Bradshaw had died abruptly thirteen years before, practically to the day Liberman died. And it would have been her brother Gerald's 59th birthday, whose death in that car-bike accident in 1951 left the Win-tours in emotional turmoil.

Anna attended the Costume Institute Gala, which she cochaired at New York's Metropolitan Museum of Art, on December 6, just a week before her father's funeral service. That year was a significant occasion because the institute was launching a new display of rock and roll clothing. Henry and Nancy Kissinger, Ahmet and Mica Ertegun, Prince Pavlos and Princess Marie-Chantal of Greece, Jerry Seinfeld, Jennifer Love Hewitt, Elizabeth Hurley, Debbie Harry, Kate Moss, Elle Macpherson, Donatella Versace, and Calvin Klein were among those in attendance.

Yet there in the center ring was Anna, with all of the salacious attention centered on her, crying in public with mascara streaming down her cheeks, her tear-filled swollen eyes hidden behind her sunglasses. Some assumed she was furious because Shelby Bryan had to leave the party early on the night that was supposed to be their first public appearance since divorcing. Whitney Houston, who had her own marital issues with her husband, Bobby Brown, was cited as saying that Anna was so angry that she would "screw that boyfriend up!" "

Anna had fallen apart that sparkling evening due to the deaths of her father and Alex Liberman, as well as the roller-coaster ride of her affair.

"Anna felt as if a dark cloud had dropped over her and would not lift," recalls a friend who met her in London for her father's burial service.

Hundreds of VIPs, celebrities, and media attended Wintour's life celebration on December 13 at London's Royal Opera House's Vilar Floral Hall. Shelby Bryan was among them, but David Shaffer was not.

Anna spoke warmly about her father and, for the first time in anyone's memory, sympathetically about how his second wife had made the last two decades of his life joyful. At least outwardly, there appeared to be some type of reconciliation. Patrick, Anna's brother, was said to have written her speech.

"I was abruptly struck by how closely she reminded me of her father in voice and demeanor," said journalist Paul Callan, who began out in newspapers working for Charles Wintour. I assumed it was Charles speaking when I closed my eyes."

Anna posed for a photo with family members after the service. She was the only one who smiled for the camera, as if she were walking down the red carpet at an awards ceremony. Susan Summers, who had previously worked for Charles Wintour at the Evening Standard, approached Anna, who was wrapped in mink, to express her condolences and utter a few kind things about her father. "I stretched out, and she recoiled—recoiling! I'm not sure if she was expecting me to paint her mink or not, but she recoiled physically. She resembles the queen. You're not supposed to approach her."

Anna and her husband divorced in New York in the new millennium, with the papers sealed by the court. But, according to a friend of the marriage, "Anna was quite kind with David," while Anna's brother Jim told Vivienne Lasky, "Anna got to keep two properties."

On March 10, 2000, Katherine Bryan filed for divorce in Manhattan Supreme Court, alleging "adultery" and "cruel and unusual treatment." Five days later, Bryan sued her in Houston, three days after their eighteenth wedding anniversary. He felt it would be more financially advantageous for him to get the divorce in Texas, despite the fact that he owned three residences in New York, because that's where their prenuptial agreement was negotiated and signed, and it was covered by Texas community property law. Furthermore, because Texas had no-fault divorce, the specifics of his affair with Anna would not be made public. Don Fullenweider, his Houston lawyer, claimed his client was more of a Texan than a New Yorker. "He's a fifth-generation Texan," said the lawyer. He noted that, in addition to New York, Bryan had property "everywhere," controlled an oil company in Houston and was a member of the posh River Oaks Country Club, and owned a ranch in Brewster County. Bernard Clair, his wife's lawyer, believed that New York was the right place. The lawyers fought on, putting in long hours.

Bryan urged the court to enforce the prenup as part of his divorce suit. Katherine Bryan agreed to seek no more than half of the community property and no interest or part of his separate property under it. The prenup also included a number of options. The first was for him to pay her $900,000 in cash. The other was a sum equal to 10% of his after-tax net wealth in excess of ten million dollars, payable in four equal annual installments. A condition provided for identical alimony payments and $50,000 in child support per year until their children reached the age of eighteen.

Bryan was estimated to be worth $30 million at the time he met Anna. However, in August 2000, he resigned from his lucrative post as chairman and CEO of ICG Communications, a nationwide phone and data network operator. Between the spring of 2000 and the day of his resignation, the business stock, of which Bryan controlled 2.3 million shares, fell from $39 to $6.47, a loss of $75 million on paper. According to the New York Daily News, "it appears like some form of karma just caught up with" Bryan. "With the changed circumstances, it'll be interesting to watch how long Bryan remains in Wintour's good graces."

Despite her financial situation, Anna reportedly vacationed with Bryan in the south of France that summer, with her two children and his two boys.

Then, in November 2000, ICG Communications, a high-flying company, filed for Chapter 11 bankruptcy protection. According to press sources, the corporation was deeply in debt. Class action lawsuits were filed alleging that Bryan and others defrauded investors, which Bryan disputed.

Regardless, he was still wealthy, and he and Katherine Bryan divorced after reaching an agreement. Their townhouse, which Bill Clinton famously entertained at a Democratic fund-raiser, was reportedly sold for $11 million, and the former Mrs. Bryan relocated to Park Avenue.

Anna appeared more relaxed and less frigid with Bryan than she had with David Shaffer, much as Audrey Slaughter had made Charles Wintour a happier and less icy guy when she hooked up with him. She lightened and emphasized her distinctive bob, and she used her sunglasses less in public. There was even discussion that she appeared younger than she was—a nip and tuck here and there wasn't out of the question. At the New Yorkers for Children Fall Gala, Anna and Bryan danced to the Village People's disco gay song "YMCA," and the boyish Bryan grabbed Gwyneth Paltrow and Oscar de la Renta and danced with them.

The divorce of Anna appears to have had little emotional impact on her children. "Bee and Charlie live in a world of acquaintances whose parents have affairs, whose names wind up in the gossip pages, who divorce," a family observer observes. They simply saw it as a way of life."

Anna and her daughter have always had a tight relationship—the girl attended her first design show with her mother when she was in her terrible twos—and some were later convinced that Bee Shaffer, as one fashion wag put it, "is Anna squared sans the shades and the bob."

By the age of ten, the two didn't agree on fashion. "She doesn't listen to anything I say," Anna grumbled. "She prefers overalls and sweatpants, but not dresses." That's good as long as she's happy, but every now and again, I'd like her to wear a dress."

The girl frequently confronted Anna as she dressed for an evening out, claiming that what she was wearing was "too exposing." "She'd like me to go out like a monk," Anna explained.

All of that changed when she entered her teen years and became a "beautiful young fashion plate in her own right," according to one fashion journalist. She wore a "flattering, dreamy, frothy, pale strapless full skirted tulle gown" to an event on the arm of Olivier Theyskens, who designed for Rochas.

When Condé Nast decided to enter the pop tart sector with a fashion and style magazine focused at young girls called Teen Vogue in the spring of 2003, sixteen-year-old Bee Shaffer was named a contributing editor—nepotism, like wearing fur, had never been a problem for Anna. Anna considered girls who couldn't see over the edge of a runway to be aspiring fashionistas. "They are aware of media coverage. . . They are far more aware of current fashion trends than girls used to be. And that is why the magazine exists."

Anna's daughter was involved in the first issue, according to Amy Astley, the magazine's editor and Anna's protégée. "I agree with everything Bee says. She is clearly the ideal Teen Vogue reader. She and her buddies make an excellent focus group. They're smart and sophisticated, and they obviously know a lot about fashion, yet they're still regular girls."

Anna and her sleek, shiny-haired, and curvy daughter, who has been described as the Vogue editor-in-"mini-me," chief's sit together in the front row at fashion shows on occasion and occasionally attend cocktail parties together.

According to a Wintour family friend, publicist Paul Wilmot, Anna's daughter has "the Genes and, through osmosis, she's got the exposure and experience." . . . Expect her to end up as a young editor someplace."

Perhaps the next hot model in America.

By mid-2004, there was speculation that numerous agencies were interested in representing Bee, but she was set on attending college, something her mother had not done.

Anna was overjoyed that her divorce was finally over. Vogue was still number one, and Anna was in complete command. And she had Bryan all to herself now.

Then she learned that her long standing adversary, Tina Brown, who is now the editor of gossipy Talk magazine, was preparing to strike, having assigned a "grudge" profile of Bryan. Brown had left enemies behind when she left Condé Nast to launch Talk. Anna was first on the list.

"Tina has a really visceral dislike for Anna," a close watcher of the two ladies reveals. "It was not based on logic or anything Anna did to her, but rather on the intrinsic rivalry that would develop between these two extremely determined and uncompromising British editors."

According to the insider, Brown targeted Bryan in particular since Brown's husband, editor Harry Evans, allegedly had affairs. "Tina was quite upset about it and was wondering why no one was focusing on other editors who had problematic marriages." Tina was quite bitter—not only about the negative publicity, but also about her husband's womanizing—because there had always been material about Harry, blind items in the tabloids about him. So there's Anna fooling around with Shelby, and Tina can't wait to do a story in Talk about it. It appeared to be a grudge piece."

Another factor in Brown's decision to go after Anna by publishing a story about Bryan was the fact that Vanity Fair (Condé Nast) writer Judith Bachrach was working on an unofficial biography about her marriage. She expected the book about her life with Evans to be a smear job.

"Even though Bryan made for a real news story, Anna was over herself when she found out about the Talk peace and made a flurry of phone calls to Brown begging her not to run the story," a publishing insider adds. "Brown assured her not to worry, but that she intended to pursue the story further." Anna phoned every media power person she knew in an attempt to have the item killed. According to what I've heard, she pleaded with Graydon Carter [Vanity Fair's editor] and went to Si [Newhouse] to see if he could help.``

The Guardian in London, where Patrick Wintour worked, leapt on the feud between the two British magazine queens, noting that Brown "heartlessly rebuffed Anna's pleas not to run an exposé of Anna's arm-candy." . . They have a long history of animosity."

"Full of Texas charm, Shelby Bryan garnered over $3 billion from investors as clever as John Malone, wooed Vogue editor Anna Wintour, and gathered millions for the Democratic Party." Then his firm failed. The losers are left wondering if he intentionally misled them—or whether love and ambition distracted him."

There was a full-page portrait of the former Golden Gloves fighter, hands on his hips in his pinstriped two-button business suit, ready to fight anyone.

On the contents page, a sunglassed Anna in a slinky off-the-shoulder gown stood next to a tuxedoed Bryan. "Last June, having just returned from a trip in the south of France with his girlfriend, Vogue editor in chief Anna Wintour," started the tale, which was intended to be about Bryan's business methods. . .”

The story mentioned the affair and quoted other women who complained about Bryan's "louche behavior."

Bachrach quips in her book, "Tina was kind enough to give Wintour a copy of the published article, with a 'With Compliments' card attached."

Brown had really done what appeared to the media to be another number on Anna, and she was undoubtedly out for vengeance.

Bryan and Anna did not take legal action against Brown's magazine for the article, but Bryan was successful in pursuing a libel claim against the London Daily Telegraph, which had picked up material from the Talk piece under the headline "English Queens of New York in Clash over Wintour's Boyfriend" five months after its piece ran. In a published story, the newspaper apologized to Bryan and pledged to make a large donation to a charity of his choice as well as pay his legal bills.

The fashion website Chic Happens, which broke the tale of the affair, remarked that "Britain's more liberal libel rules" made a ruling in Bryan's favor "more possible," and that "a triumph in the UK—the home soil of both Wintour and Brown—would be that much sweeter."

Anna began another love affair, this time with the glitterati of Houston, her lover's homeland, where the gorgeous twosome began making stopovers and Anna was welcomed like visiting royalty. Anna and Bryan's openly amorous behavior also fueled rumors and gossip. Bryan and Anna acted like a pair of going-steady adolescents at a spin-the-bottle party at his brother's party at the prestigious Bayou Club, which includes high-powered members such as George W. Bush.

"In front of the world, Shelby and Anna spent a big part of this party making out, tongues down each other's throats, seated on a bench in a little entrance to the party room," claims an informed Houston social watcher.

Anna became friends with a number of the city's wealthiest and most prominent fashionistas, women who read Vogue as meticulously as they do a prenuptial agreement, fashion horses who spend tens of thousands of dollars a year on designer duds.

Becca Cason Thrash, a gorgeous fifty-something wife of one of the city's gazillionaires who had to expand her closet by more than a thousand square feet to fit all of her elegant Chanel, Lacroix, Helmut Lang, Stella McCartney, Gianfranco Ferre, Sergio Rossi, Marc Bouwer, Jean Paul Gaultier, and La Perla, was one with whom Anna eventually bonded. She had everything. This daughter of a Harlington, Texas, TV sportscaster who married right was a boldface name in Houston—and in New York and Paris—having been written about in the Houston Chronicle, Women's Wear Daily, Town and

Country, Tina Brown's Talk before it went defunct, and Harper's Bazaar, where the fashion diva was profiled as one of "Couture's Big Spenders."

She was dubbed "the high priestess of posh" and "TriBecca" because she changed her beautiful, gorgeous dresses three times during the opulent parties she held at her twenty-thousand-square-foot mansion: indoor pool, two-thousand-square-foot kitchen, glass-floored second story. The location was formerly described as resembling a "cutting-edge art museum."

"Anna really loves Texas, she loves it," exclaims Thrash, who had invited Anna to be the guest of honor for a Houston Stages Repertory Theater celebration at her home, an evening that included a shortened performance of Full Gallop, a. Diana Vreeland, Vogue's former editor, is the subject of a one-woman show.

"We on the theater board were brainstorming different ways to really make the evening special, and we came up with the idea of bringing Anna," Thrash explains. "There's no resemblance between Anna and Diana Vreeland other than the fact that they both held the same job," she says. Anna in no way compares herself to Mrs. Vreeland."

Another Houston fashion powerhouse, Susan Criner, who was a personal friend of Bryan and his mother, handled the arrangements for Anna's royal visit. "Susan and Gretchen were so close that when Gretchen died, a lot of her Chanel couture and a lot of her Chanel clothes went to her," Thrash explains. Susan still keeps and wears them."

Thrash claims she felt "intimidated" by Anna until the dazzling night of the huge party. "I'm not easily intimidated, but there are no words to convey how much Anna, her demeanor, intimidated me. I was intimidated whenever I saw her at couture or the fashion show. She'd walk in with her famous sunglasses on and grab the nicest seat in the house, and I'd say to myself, 'God, she's a very imposing, intimidating figure.' You know who I'm talking about. She is well-known throughout the world. Everyone recognizes Anna Wintour as the most powerful woman in the world of fashion."

She couldn't fathom it all, so Anna became a terrifying figure to her.

Politicians, celebrities, and designers looked to be in attendance at Thrash's party, as did everyone who was someone in Texas and the fashion industry. Trash erected custom lighting to give the walls a crimson tinge, and models were hired to circulate among the attendees wearing clothes by the designers that were present, including Mark Badgley, James Mischka, and Diane von Furstenberg. One woman was overheard moaning about her "jewelry elbow," reportedly due to the weight of all the bracelets and rocks she was wearing.

Anna, dressed in a silvery Chanel suit but without the sunglasses, arrived late and holding hands with Bryan. Every eye was on her. The local press had said very little about their adulterous romance. In Houston, such gossip is rarely published. Before the things run, lawyers threaten to sue. But everyone in Thrash's large circle knew everything there was to know about Anna and talked about it all the time. One of the attendees observed that Anna's eyes blinked quickly without her spectacles and that she performed a double take when she saw the ample new breasts of a Texan rose in a low-cut Ralph Lauren gown who introduced herself, virtually bowing to the editrix from New York.

When they shared the honor table that night, the once-afraid Thrash bonded with her imperiousness.

"It was just the eight of us," Thrash adds, "Anna and Bryan, the Thrashes, the Criners, and Bryan's brother and sister-in-law, and we spent three or four hours at the same table and interacted, and I just felt Anna was amazing, and I was no longer intimidated." "Anna was delightful, yet she is completely and utterly misunderstood." It's just that she's a slow starter. I believe she is extremely British, very reserved, and for a Texan, this might be misconstrued.

"In my events, I never seat people who are sleeping together next to each other, so I seated Anna between my husband and J.P." So my husband was her dinner companion, and he enjoyed her, thought she was fantastic and very sexy—not in a blatant, but in a subtle manner."

Thrash's adoring companion stood up to speak with another partygoer, and Bryan, "who is so extremely effervescent and fun, raced over and sat in his chair as fast as he could, and Anna and Shelby leaned over and kissed," Thrash recalls warmly. "They're like a newlywed couple in love." After all of the speeches and presentations, Anna and Bryan were the first to hit the dance floor. My girlfriend was dancing next to them and told me, "God, they were kissing, and he was all over her."

Anna, who had never had a true prom, was at her massive desk in her enormous corner office with a wall of glass that provided her a wonderful view of Times Square from the new Condé Nast tower the following Monday.

She was at the pinnacle of her career and her life, ready to begin work on another lushly beautiful, catalog-thick, extremely lucrative, style-setting, sexy-celebrity-on-the-cover issue of Vogue.

And, as always, she was ready to fight with her opponent and emerge victorious.

Her relationship with Bryan was still golden at the middle of the first decade of the new millennium. They were photographed holding hands at fashion presentations, cocktail parties, and cultural events in New York. Yet when the photographers arrived, Bryan usually faded into the background, putting Anna in the forefront. Their affair was no longer regarded as breaking news and had long since faded from the gossip columns.

Yet, in May 2004, their relationship was once again the subject of tabloid speculation. The headline on the New York Post's Page Six read, "Anna, Lover in 'Illegal' Sublet." The story claimed that Bryan was unlawfully subletting an enormous $5,800-per-month rooftop loft from internationally recognized hairdresser John Frieda. A woman whose family owned the loft building claimed Frieda had moved out and had been "replaced by Bryan and Win-tour," and when she confronted them, "they froze." By this point, Anna had received her letter from Frieda's old mailbox, which she instantly body-slammed shut and attempted to hide into the wall. She got away with it since she's so little. Shelby then stated in a faux British accent, 'We're only staying here for one or two days,' and Anna and her partner headed out for a night on the town."

Anna had the best photographers working for her at Vogue, including the incomparable Helmut Newton, whose erotically charged, fascinating, and gorgeous fashion photographs had long been an asset to the magazine. He was regarded as the father of "porno chic."

Newton was still under contract at the age of eighty-three and had been sending ideas to Anna from his house in Monte Carlo for a layout he planned to do for her in Los Angeles in 2003.

They had a close working relationship since the late 1970s, when Anna was fashion editor at Viva.

"We had our times over the years." "Anna and I had many moments," Newton says, remembering how "difficult, demanding, and stubborn Anna can be." But she was always sure of herself. She knew when to pay attention. Her success was not solely due to her charisma.

"We had several disagreements concerning her choosing of my photographs. Anna might be difficult, but I've always admired her. Vogues her publication, and she is an expert on the job. She mostly makes me proud. Nobody can compete with her. She'll continue selecting what's in and out of style long after I'm gone."

Not long after Newton, dubbed "King of Kink" for his erotic photographs, arrived in the City of Angels, disaster struck. On January 23, 2004, he was driving out of the Chateau Marmont hotel's garage on Sunset Boulevard when he experienced an apparent heart attack, lost control, and smashed into a wall. He passed away at Cedars-Sinai Medical Center. June, his muse and fellow photographer, had been photographing her gravely crippled husband for many years. His ashes were laid to rest in Berlin, his birthplace, on June 2.

Anna was among the world's most prominent fashionistas who paid tribute to the great man in July during a memorial service held in Paris's opulent and baroque Theatre du Palais Royale. Anna, dressed in a black-and-white Carolina Herrera gown, spoke eloquently about her time working with Newton. "A lot of surprising things happen at Vogue, but no one is as constantly scandalous as Helmut," she admitted. She referred to him as a "visionary photographer" with the ability to transform even the most mundane assignment into an exciting event. She said the photographs he gave her had left her "aghast, flabbergasted, and always amazed" over the years.

Then she shocked the audience, which included Tom Ford, Marc Jacobs, Jean Paul Gaultier, Stella McCartney, and Anna's daughter, Bee, who was dressed in one of her mother's black Prada gowns and served as an usher at the service, by revealing her one regret in an otherwise glamorous and very successful life. Helmut Newton had volunteered to photograph her as a young fashion editor at Harpers & Queen, but the shoot had never taken place.

"I would have loved to have been one of Helmut's women," Anna declared. I can't think of a higher praise than being considered worthy of Helmut's lens."

The event's grief, however, gave way to excitement as a result of fantastic news from America.

Si Newhouse informed her that the September 2004 issue of Vogue would be the largest ever, as well as the largest monthly magazine in publishing history, at 832 pages. When Anna Wintour approached her quarter-century anniversary as editor in chief, it was evident that she had genuinely transformed Vogue into the world's most significant and successful fashion arbiter and glamor page-turner.

Printed in Great Britain
by Amazon

28053003R00082